It Ain't Trickin'
If
You Got It

Part Two

Novel By:

First Lady K

It Ain't Trickin' If You Got It 2

First Lady K

It Ain't Trickin' If You Got It 2 © 2015. By Kirsten Bailey

First Lady K

Text ROYALTY to 42828 to join our mailing list!

ROYALTY is looking for aspiring authors in the areas of Urban Fiction, Urban Romance & Interracial Romance. If you are looking for an independent publishing company, submit the first 3 – 4 chapters of your completed manuscript to submissions@royaltypublishinghouse.com.

PREFACE

"What's the matter, Alexis?" Keisha asked. "Cat got your tongue?" she said

Alexis lay on the floor covered in old and new blood with her right eye swollen shut. Fresh tears formed in her eyes and it stung her face as they fell. She had lost track of the time that she had been there.

"See, before you were popping off at the mouth on the phone and shit to me, tryna tell Henderson how he needs to check me. Well, here I am, Alexis. Check me. Oh wait, you can't," she said with a sinister laugh. She leaned forward and whispered in her ear, "You can't do shit but lay there. I'm gonna enjoy watching Shawn fuck you up, bitch. By the time we're done with you, you'll wish you died a quick death." She spat on her face and slammed the door shut.

Alexis cried slowly and prayed to God it would be over soon and that he would just let her die.

CHAPTER ONE

Alexis snapped back from her thoughts of that night. She sat in her therapist's office in a chair and listened to the doctor asking her questions, irritated. She had been coming to Dr. Rhimes for almost two years since she was kidnapped. The school suggested that she see a therapist after she came back to school for the start of her senior year and she had an episode in class one day and attacked a girl that she thought was trying to hurt her. Alexis did so much damage that it took four university officers to subdue her. She was expelled from school and not allowed back until she had undergone medical attention and been cleared to return. She had two more weeks of therapy left until she received the clearance that she needed to start the upcoming spring semester. Alexis was ready to return so she said just enough to please her doctor. She still had not talked about what happened to her or being kidnapped, but she was still cooperative. Alexis looked at the clock behind Dr. Rhimes to see she only had twelve minutes left in her session. Dr. Rhimes looked at Alexis, concerned.

"Are you alright, Alexis?" he asked.

"Yeah, I'm good." Alexis sighed as she pushed a few wisps of hair out of her face.

Dr. Rhimes looked at her over his glasses. "Okay then. Well, tell me what is going on in your mind right now."

"As far as what?" Alexis asked with a tone of agitation.

"Are you ready to return to school? I know your senior year is important," he said.

Alexis was ready to go but, she knew she had to be careful so that the doctor would sign off on her going back.

"Yeah, I am. It's senior year so I'm ready to graduate," Alexis answered.

"Any plans after graduation?" Dr. Rhimes asked.

"Well, I was thinking about moving back home and trying to work for the county with children," Alexis said.

"Really?" Dr. Rhimes asked, genuinely interested. "What kind of work do you want to do with children?"

Alexis answered proudly, "I was thinking about working with children that have had traumatic experiences."

Dr. Rhimes took his glasses off and closed his book of notes on his client. "Well, I'm sure that you will do great at it. Alright, Alexis, our time is up for today but, I want you to do something for me in the next couple of days until we see each other again. Is that okay?" he asked

"Okay, what is it?" Alexis asked.

"Anytime you feel stressed, if at all, I want you to sit back, close your eyes and completely relax. Either before you get out of the bed in the morning, or before you go to sleep, maybe even throughout the day. Just take a few minutes to close your eyes. Close your eyes and relax your entire body. Let your mind just wander away. As it wanders, I want you to take deep breaths and release slowly. Imagine you're looking at a glass of water. As you are taking the deep breaths, imagine that glass of water slowly pouring out the water, along with the negativity that you may have experienced during the day," he instructed Alexis.

Alexis picked up her purse and keys and headed to the door.

"Alexis," Dr. Rhimes called after her.

Alexis turned to the doctor. "Yes?" she asked.

"I know you've gone through a lot. I'm going to help you the best that I can, ok?" Dr. Rhimes told her.

Alexis thought about how nice the doctor was being. "I know," she said, giving him a light smile and walking out the door.

*

Damn, it seems like I been here forever, Ariane thought to herself. She sat in her Nissan Altima parked across from the medical center waiting for Alexis to come out. She had been sitting there for almost two hours watching and waiting. *What the hell is she doing in there?* she wondered.

Ariane had spent the last few weeks following Alexis whenever she could. She thought about Jayshawn being in prison for the last eight months awaiting his appeal for kidnapping and rape, and she knew she was doing the right thing. When he first got arrested, she had been going to the jail every weekend to visit and she'd paid his attorney like he told her to. She hadn't gone to the prison in almost four months but made sure to continue to pay his attorney. She wrote him letters letting him know that she was coming for a visit soon but she had business to handle. She didn't want to let him know too much because she didn't want him to get mad at her for going after this girl.

I don't understand what the fuck he sees in this bitch, she thought. This bitch doesn't even wanna be with him and fucking got him locked up chasing after her stupid ass.

Ariane couldn't understand why Jayshawn was so stuck on her. From what he told her, she lied to the cops after coming in his apartment and starting a fight with his baby mama. He told her he did cheat and fuck her, but that she lied about being raped and held against her will and she forgave him even though he blamed her.

She didn't listen to him that day and they got into an argument. She vowed to do whatever he needed and wanted to make it up to him. She sat in the parking area across the street and thought about everything that happened over the last few months. The more she thought about it, the angrier she became. She placed her hand on her stomach and reassured herself and her unborn child everything would be okay.

Ariane was about to call it a day when she saw Alexis exiting the ground level entrance and walking towards the lower level parking deck.

"Perfect time," she said out loud as she got out her car and headed to put her plan in motion.

*

Alexis walked to her car in the parking garage of her therapist's office with her car keys in her hand. As she was walking, she heard something behind her so she quickened her pace. She hit the unlock button on the remote of her car and started the ignition as she continued to walk to her car. She looked over her shoulder and saw no one but continued to walk quickly. Hearing the noise again, she ran to her car, jumping in and locking her door. She didn't realize until she was safely in her car that she was holding her breath.

Gasping for air, Alexis pulled a bottle of Xanax out of her glove box. Her doctor had prescribed her the pills for her anxiety a few months prior. The prescription had run out but she had a friend that worked in the pharmacy that was able to give her the pills that she needed. She knew she shouldn't be taking them, but right now her mind was racing a mile a minute. She couldn't shake the negative thoughts she was having. *All over a nigga!* she thought.

Alexis popped the pills and started her car, exiting the parking deck to head home.

*

2003

She replayed that night over and over in her head. She remembered Keisha laughing as she begged for her life through swollen lips. Whenever Keisha would leave the room, Jayshawn would come in, lock the door and torture her by forcing himself on her. Alexis recalled him coming into the room and opening the closet door where she had been laying for what seemed like forever. He stood over her and dragged her outside of the closet so that her legs were stretched out on the floor. Alexis groaned in agony, hoping he wouldn't take advantage. She turned her head and noticed there was an alarm clock on the nightstand. She saw that the clock read 3:37pm so she knew he would be there a while.

Alexis lay on the floor praying that he wouldn't hurt her as she watched Jayshawn pull his pants down and force himself on her.

The pain was unbelievable and fresh tears fell down her face and cheeks. He continued to please himself, all the while telling her how he knew she was enjoying it and how good she felt. He pumped harder the more she tried to fight. He gripped her throat and eventually she stopped fighting and cried silently. She closed her eyes and just hoped to God he would finish soon. Alexis looked over at the clock and watched the numbers change. When he finished, it was 6:19pm. He stood up, pulled his pants up and walked over to his bed. He sat down and opened the drawer to the nightstand. He pulled out a blunt and lit it as she lay there sore and in pain.

He took a slow drag of the blunt and let it out. He sighed as if he was tired and leaned back against his headboard. He put his feet up and looked over at Alexis laying on the floor in the fetal position.

"You wanna hit?" he asked her.

Alexis lay there not responding. She knew that he wasn't serious because the minute the tape came off; she was going to start screaming. She'd done it two days before and Keisha hit her so hard she was unconscious most of the day. She lay there quiet and afraid.

"So you not gonna answer me, huh?" Jayshawn asked her. "It's cool. You should be nice to me. Keisha wants to just get rid of you. See, I'm keeping you alive." He shook his head as he continued to fill the room with the scent of marijuana.

"All you had to do was just give me what I wanted." he went on. "But you just had to tease me. I almost thought you were a good

15

girl. But, then you start bringing these niggas around here and I knew I would get you. It was only a matter of time. But you tried to be all cute and shit and get a fucking boyfriend. It's just icing on the fucking cake that your boyfriend is her fucking baby daddy. But I got a little secret for you." He got up and walked over to Alexis lying on the floor and kneeled down. "As soon as that nigga come back, I'm gonna get rid of him, and I'm gonna get rid of her, too, and me and you really gonna have some fun then." He stroked her face and she flinched feeling his finger on her.

The door opened and Keisha walked in texting on her phone. She looked up to see Jayshawn on the floor beside Alexis.

"What the fuck are you doing?" she asked him angrily.

Jayshawn ignored her and got up, walking to his bed to sit down. "Chill the fuck out. I was putting tape on the bitch mouth," he told her.

Keisha walked over and kicked Alexis in the stomach, causing her to groan in pain. "Then why is the tape wet?" she spat at him.

Jayshawn sighed and looked at Keisha as if she was the dumbest chic on the planet. "You really need to get your shit together, Keisha. Do you not see the tears on her face? Obviously, she's been crying. Damn, how dumb can you be?" he mumbled as he got ready to put Alexis back in the closet.

Keisha blocked him from doing that. "Hold up. Why the fuck does it smell like latex in here?" she asked him and walked over to the trash can to see the empty condom wrapper.

Jayshawn seemed unfazed. "I mean, well, shit. She here, so why not?" he asked smugly.

Keisha became very angry. "What the fuck? Have you lost your mind? Bad enough you insist on keeping the bitch around, but now you wanna fuck this bitch?! Is that why you want to keep her around? Huh?" she said to him.

Jayshawn simply looked at her and lit his blunt. "Shut the fuck up," he spat. "Shut the fuck up and go do what I told you to do fucking three hours ago. Did you text that nigga and convince him to bring his ass over here?" he yelled at her.

Keisha flinched at the sound of him raising his voice. "Yes, baby. I did. But he was saying that if it didn't have anything to do with Tee Tee that he didn't want to talk to me," she told him, immediately calming down.

Jayshawn looked at her as if he couldn't understand the language that she was speaking. "So then why the fuck didn't you tell him it was about your damn daughter? Do you want me to do all of this shit by my damn self? Because if I do, then you can get the fuck out now," he told her.

Keisha walked over to Jayshawn and attempted to straddle him. "Baby, that's not it. You know I'm in it with you. I would do anything you ask, you know that," she pleaded with him.

"Then act like it," he told her.

He pushed her off him and walked over towards the bathroom. Keisha sat for a minute and thought about what she was about to do. As much as she hated Henderson for not wanting to be with her, she didn't want Jayshawn to kill him either. She knew she couldn't take care of their daughter better than he could because she really didn't want her. But at this point, it was either do what she was told or she would piss Jayshawn off and there's no telling what he would do. Jayshawn went into the bathroom and Keisha picked up her phone to text Henderson.

Keisha: Hey we need to meet up. Got some stuff my mom got for Tee Tee.

She put her phone down and saw Alexis looking at her. She felt herself getting angry all over again and looked to see if Jayshawn was looking. She walked over to the closet area where Alexis lay and kicked her in her stomach; hard. Alexis groaned in pain and tears began to fall down her face. Keisha grabbed her by her hair and shoved her back into the closet.

"Fucking bitch. You had to come along and fuck shit up. You thought I wasn't gonna find you? Huh, bitch?" she asked as she knelt down in front of her, whispering so that Jayshawn wouldn't hear her.

She pulled out a small switchblade she kept in her back pocket. Alexis' eyes grew large in fear of what could happen. "That's right bitch. I can end you right now." She trailed the blade down the side of Alexis face. "Don't underestimate me, bitch." Alexis cried harder and tried to move away from Keisha's grasp.

Keisha heard Jayshawn flush the toilet and got up, walking back over towards the bed so as to not to raise suspicion with him. He walked over to the bed and lay down and grabbed Keisha, pulling her to him.

"You wanna make it up to me?" he asked her.

Keisha smiled. "Yes."

Jayshawn pulled her head towards his shorts and lay back so that she could apologize the way he wanted. He looked over to see Alexis laying on the floor and smiled as he imagined it was her lips he was feeling.

*

All through her drive home, Alexis thought about the events that had happened in her life in the past year. She thought about how much her life had changed. She felt the tears start to well in her eyes as she continued to head home. She pushed the phone button on her car dash to make a phone call without having to look for her phone.

"Call babe," she said.

"Calling babe," the system confirmed as it dialed. After a few rings, the call connected.

"Hello?" a deep, familiar voice responded.

"Hey, babe. I'm on the way home and should be there in about ten minutes," Alexis said.

"Okay," he responded. "I just took the food out of the oven so everything will be ready by the time you get here. Honk when you get outside and I will come get you," he told her.

"Babe, it's okay. You don't have to walk me to and from my car all the time," she said. "Not to say I don't appreciate it, but I am going to have to try to find some level of normalcy."

"I know that," he told her. "But I want to make sure that nothing or nobody bothers you. Besides, I have to walk Chub Chub anyway."

Alexis smirked. "Please. You always manage to have to take him for a walk when I'm coming home? Okay, I'm gonna let you think you won," she said with a laugh.

Alexis could hear him laughing on the other end of the phone. "Oh, I always win. Now hurry up and come on, woman. I'm hungry," he said joking.

"I'm pulling up into the parking lot now," she informed him as she turned into her complex in a now gated community.

She drove up to the gate to scan her gate card for entrance. The gates opened and she turned the corner to head towards her building. Pulling up, she saw her boyfriend walking with her dog Chub Chub. She smiled as she parked her car and he came over, opening the door for her. She got out with her dog wagging his tail vigorously and licking her from excitement. She bent down to pet him and closed and locked her car door.

"Well, hello there, Mr. Strong," Alexis greeted her boyfriend as he grabbed her bag for her and they headed towards her apartment.

"Hello yourself, Ms. Thomas," he said as he kissed her cheek.

The two began walking to her condo. Alexis smiled as she thought of the way her boyfriend had really been there for her through the past year. She and Henderson broke up a month after he graduated and moved to Virginia. They tried the long distance relationship but Alexis knew Henderson couldn't be faithful to her like that and she didn't want to have to check everything that he did or constantly worry as to what or who he was doing. He got mad at her when she came to visit one weekend and went through his phone to see what he had been up to. That was all she needed and she left. She was tired of it. She blamed him for her attack and ran out. They talked on the phone a few times and she apologized, but she just couldn't bring herself to work it out with him. Collin was the exact opposite of that.

Collin Strong, Jr. was someone that she never imagined herself with. He was very quiet and reserved and worked the night shift at the UPS hub so that he could go to school during the day. He was graduating in the spring so he didn't do much partying because he was all about the books. Alexis remembered the day she met him.

She was in the library studying for a test when she noticed it was getting dark outside the window. She quickly gathered her things to throw them in her bag and began to walk towards the help desk to return the books she had been using. She was rummaging through her purse for her keys with her free hand and not looking at where she was going when she missed the one step that connected the lobby to the walkway of the reference hall. Alexis fell, dropping everything she had in her hands.

"Ah!" Alexis screamed as she fell feeling excruciating pain in her ankle.

One of the girls that worked in the computer lab downstairs ran up to help her up. Barely weighing 100 pounds, she looked around to see if anyone could help. Collin came around the corner with one of his fraternity brothers and saw Alexis on the floor. He quickly approached to see if he could help.

"Are you okay?" he asked.

"Yeah, for the most part," Alexis responded. "I think I may have sprained my ankle though."

Collin leaned down to help her up. "Here; put your arm around my neck and we'll get you up," he instructed her.

Alexis put her arm around him while the assistant picked her belongings up off the floor for her. Collin picked her up easily and carried her over to the chair to sit her down. The assistant sat her stuff down on the table and pulled out her cell phone.

"I'm going to call student health services and see if they can get someone over here to come and look at it," the girl said.

Alexis objected before she could dial out. "No, it's ok. It's just a sprain. I'll be okay," she said, putting her books bag in her bag. "I just needed to return this and I guess I wasn't paying attention," she said, handing the girl the book that she had borrowed from the reference desk.

The girl took the book and placed it on a nearby cart. "Are you sure you don't want me to call anybody?" she asked. "Maybe one of your friends or a family member?"

"Yea, because you can't walk on this foot," Collin interjected.

Alexis appreciated his concern but people were starting to gather and she didn't want to bring too much more attention to herself than there already was.

"Tell you what, I'm going to go get my car and take you home," he said.

Alexis shook her head no. "No, you don't have to do that," she said.

"I know, but I want to. I'll be right back," he said as he walked out of the library to get his car.

Alexis sat and waited, pulling out her phone and checking to see if she had any missed messages or calls. She had a voicemail from an unknown number that sounded like one of the foreign telemarketers. She deleted the message without listening to it in its entirety. Sighing, she put her phone back in her bag and waited for Collin. A few minutes later, Collin re-entered the library and helped Alexis stand up.

"All right, take your time. I pulled up right at the door so, you can either put your arm around my neck and we'll walk slowly, or I can just pick you up and carry you to the car," he instructed her. Alexis thought about the distance it would take her to get to her car and decided to accept Collin's offer. Collin lifted her and helped her to his car.

"I really appreciate this," Alexis told Collin as he drove her home. "Do you need gas money or anything?" she asked.

"No, it's okay. I gotta head this way anyway," he told her. "And it's no problem. I'm glad I could help."

Alexis smiled and sat back as he continued to drive. "Well, again I appreciate it. Just make a left up here and my house will be the third entrance on the right." Collin nodded to acknowledge her directions. "I think I've seen you around campus before. You're an Alpha, right?" she asked him.

"Yup," he told her. "A Phi. They call me Big Brother Ghost." He smiled.

Alexis looked intrigued. "Dare I ask what that means?" she asked.

"Trust me, you don't wanna know. But I've seen you, though. I think you and your home girl came to one of our parties a while back," he said as he turned into her entrance and drove up to the gate.

"Oh yea I do remember that party last year. I left early that night. I remember I came with my best friend Summer and she was tryna get some guy that night." Alexis waited for the guard to come to the car window so she could show her license for entrance into the community.

"Good evening, Ms. Thomas," the guard greeted her. "Is everything okay?"

"Yes, it's fine, Robert. I sprained my ankle on campus and Collin here was nice enough to give me a ride home," she explained.

"Very well, Ms. Thomas." The guard stepped back and opened up the gate to allow Collin's car through.

"Let me find out you got armed security to get into your house," Collin joked as he drove in.

"Yea well, if you knew what I have been through, you would understand," she said quietly.

It was an awkward silence in the car. Collin spoke up. "Yea, I remember hearing about that. My frat brother and Henderson were roommates back in their freshman year. He told me what went down. I'm sorry you had to go through that. I mean, I know it may not mean much but, nobody deserves that kind of pain. I can't say I know what you been through because I haven't, but I commend you for even being here. It shows your strength." He pulled up in front of her house.

Alexis held her head down so that Collin couldn't see her face. She knew she was on the brink of crying so she wanted to head inside before he could see it. "Thanks," she replied. "I need to go inside. I need to study for my test tomorrow. Besides, if Robert sees you sitting here too long and you're not signed in, he will escort you off personally," she said, joking to lighten the mood.

Collin held his hands up in a mock surrender. "Whoa. Okay, I give," he laughed. "I don't want any trouble."

He opened his car door and got out to help her out of the car. He opened her car door and held her up as she tried to limp towards her door. She opened the door and her dog came running out, jumping all over her, causing her to lose her balance. Collin caught her and helped her inside.

"Chub Chub, outside!" Alexis fussed. Her dog was growling and his tail was wagging. Alexis watched him run outside. "I'm sorry about that. He's very hyperactive. I promise he doesn't bite," she apologized.

"It's cool. You want me to wait until he's finished? I don't mind," he told her.

"No, it's okay. You've done more than enough. I'll be fine. He'll come in soon. Go ahead and handle your business. Trust me, I will be fine," she assured him.

Collin smiled and walked towards the door. "Alright, well put my number in your phone. If you need anything, just hit me up."

"Okay. But I'm telling you, I will be fine," Alexis told him. "What's the number?"

"3-3-6, 9-8-7, 2-5-3-3," he told her.

Alexis stored the number in her phone. "Got it." She limped over to the couch and grabbed her dog whistle, blowing it to get the dog back in the house.

"Okay, well, I'm going to go ahead and get out of here. I will talk to you later," Collin told her. "Good night, Alexis," he told her.

"Good night, Collin," Alexis said with a smile.

Collin closed the door behind him and drove off.

Alexis got up and limped to the door, locking it and setting the alarm. She limped back over to her couch and sat down. Chub Chub jumped up on the couch beside her. She picked up her remote and cut the TV on. She found herself watching *Flavor of Love* on VH1. She watched, not really paying attention. She glanced at her phone and contemplated texting Collin. "No," she told herself. She turned her attention back to the television. Growing bored again, Alexis picked up her phone and texted her best friend.

Alexis: Hey girl, what you doing?

Summer: Nothing. Sitting here watching *Flavor of Love*. These hoes nasty as hell.

Alexis: Lol. I know right? This chic New York off the chain. Girl, tell me why I sprained my damn ankle?

Summer: What the hell? You aight?

Alexis: Yea girl. Fell in the damn library of all places. Lol. But some Alpha was in there and gave me a ride home.

Summer: Oh ok. You need anything?

Alexis: Nah I'm in for the night. I might need a ride to class in the morning. My car is still on campus.

Summer: Oh ok. Well I got an 8 o'clock class tomorrow so I can get you but it'll be early.

Alexis thought about being on campus three hours early and decided to just skip class. She had an eleven o'clock and a one o'clock on Tuesdays and Thursdays, and she hadn't missed any days, so she figured she could miss one day.

Alexis: Lol. Girl you know I can't get my ass up that early. I will probably just skip class.

Summer: Oh ok. You wanna go to the mall with us tomorrow?

Alexis: Who is us?

Summer: Me, you and Mika.

Alexis frowned at the thought of Tamika being around. She knew that she didn't have anything to do with what happened to her directly, but the fact that she was Jayshawn's brother was a little too close for comfort.

Alexis: Nah I'm good. I'm gonna hang and watch *Law & Order SVU* on DVD.

Summer: You gotta stop punishing her for her brother's fuck up.

Alexis: I'm not. I'm just not ready to talk to her.

Alexis hadn't spoken to Tamika since the police arrested her brother. Summer didn't even know about Tamika making a move on her. It was too much to get into and, knowing Summer, she would ask a thousand questions so she just left it alone.

Summer: Ok.

I know this chic better not have an attitude, Alexis thought.

Alexis: Aight I'm bout to hit the bed. I gotta go see my doctor some time tomorrow for this sprain. I'll text you later.

Summer: Aight.

Alexis put her phone down and thought about everything that had happened. She knew she shouldn't be so mad at Tamika because it wasn't her fault that her brother was a criminal. Alexis opened the drawer next to the couch and pulled out a pen and paper. She felt like writing.

Treatment of a Queen

I bowed to you. I bowed to you as my ruler, and thought you were my king

And I told myself that with you, I would forever be a queen.

I told myself that you would place me on a pedestal on top of this throne

And with you I would never fear my king would not leave his queen alone.

But see, my king ruled the throne all by himself

And seemed to forget he wasn't alone, and that there was someone else.

Someone else that was there to help his royal majesty

So why can't my king just see that all that is, is because of me? Me; his queen.

His queen that he loves, yet he does not trust

The same queen that feels neglected, but does what she must.

By going above and beyond her abilities to do what she can

So that her king can be happy and feel like he is the man.

The man that loves me but still cannot see

That the queen he's trying to change just wants to be free.

Free to feel like I can love my king without rules and regulations

And this same king treat me as a queen with no hesitations.

Because I am me; His queen.

His queen, not his child; his equal, not his inferior.

Someone that he sees eye to eye, heart to heart, and not feel like his superior.

A king that loves AND treats me right and has no doubt

And knows that his queen deserves a king that won't find the quickest way out.

A king that won't make me feel as if I have to bow to my knees

But rather look at me and say that he sees me for me.

So how am I your queen?

A queen is loved, honored, cherished, adorned and respected

Instead I've been treated like I'm some peasant whose broken down and neglected.

Begging you time and time again to stop the pain that you caused

Knowing that your queen is trying to please you in obeying all the laws.

These laws of love that you so much expect

And me trying to abide so that you don't regret.

But see, I still don't think you get it just yet.

As a queen, I deserve to be treated as such

But with you my king, I feel like it would be too much.

Too much for you to treat me like I deserve to be treated

Meaning treat me with love and make me feel needed.

Not needed as your doormat, but needed as your friend

Needed as your partner, and to be with you til the end.

A king should need his queen like you need air to breathe

Like my rib came from yours; like Adam needed Eve

But you see, you don't treat me as your queen

You say you love me but treat me as your enemy.

How am I your queen?

Alexis put her pen down and felt somewhat better for the first time that day. She picked up her cell phone and saw that it was almost midnight. She saw Collin's name was still open on her contact list. *What the hell?* she figured, and decided to text him.

Alexis: Hey this is Alexis. I just wanted to thank you again for helping me out today. Sorry if I'm messaging too late.

She gathered her things and got ready to head to her bedroom. Before she got to the room, her phone vibrated. She limped to her room and sat down on her bed. She grabbed the sleep shirt that lay at the end of her bed and changed. When she got comfortable in her bed, she remembered her phone had gone off. She picked up the phone and was surprised to see Collin had responded.

Collin: You are more than welcome, Ms. Thomas. I hope that you are comfortable and relaxed right now.

Alexis smiled at the thought of his concern. She found herself giggling and lay with her foot propped up, responding.

Alexis: Actually, yes I am. I have retired to my bedroom and am curled up under the covers watching TV.

Collin: You should be resting. Don't you have class tomorrow?

Alexis: That I do, sir. However, my first class is not until 11am and I am scheduling a doctor's appointment to have my ankle looked at so I think I am just going to skip it and make up the work later.

Collin: Well you shouldn't have to skip class. Tell me, Ms. Thomas, how do you plan to get to the doctor?

Alexis: I will probably just get Summer to take me.

Collin: I can come and get you if you'd like.

Alexis: No, it's okay. You have done more than enough. Besides, my doctor's office is closer to my house than campus so I don't want you to go out of your way.

Collin: I will determine what is out of my way. I don't mind and you shouldn't miss class. So how about I come pick you up, say 9:30am?

Alexis: Really, it's okay. Trust me, I will be fine. Summer will take me when she gets done.

Collin: And what time will that be?

Alexis: She's usually done on Tues and Thur around 4.

Collin: Ms. Thomas, that is too long to go without seeing a doctor. I will see you at 9:30. No argument. Call your bodyguard and tell him that I will need to get in tomorrow to pick you up.

Alexis: Are you always this persistent?

Collin: For things that matter? Yes.

Alexis: Oh I matter huh? Fine. I guess I will see you in the morning. Good night, Collin. ☺

Collin: That you shall. Good night, Ms. Thomas.

Alexis put her phone on the charger, smiling at the conversation that had occurred. She grabbed her teddy bear and drifted off to sleep with thoughts of Collin on her mind.

*

CHAPTER TWO

"On your feet, inmates! Mail call! Albertson, Alberto, Banks, Beauford, Bing, Blackson, Brown, Charles, Cheston, Cheston... CHESTON! Cheston, you have two seconds to be on your feet or you get a week in the hole!" Officer Morrison yelled.

Jayshawn sat unfazed in his cell as he listened to the guard yell his name and demand him up. He knew he was risking a week in the hole, but he didn't care. *If anything, it'll give me more time to think on how to get out of here,* he thought to himself. Plus, he had the admiration of so many of the inmates, his name was well-known. He sat there on his cot reading his magazine he'd taken from his cellmate. Jayshawn had not been there long but made sure that he was recognized as top dog. His cellmate was cool but Jayshawn could tell he was a follower. And that was fine with him, as long as Jayshawn was the one leading.

The guard entered the cell and snatched Jayshawn up by his jumper.

"Cheston, I know you heard me calling your name! Do you think we are supposed to wait for you? You think the sun rises and sets on you, inmate? Well, it don't, so get your ass up!" the guard yelled at him, causing the other inmates to look into the cell.

Jayshawn stood there under the guards grip with a smirk on his face. Officer Morrison stepped back and threw the mail on his bed.

"You better be glad I'm in a good mood today, inmate. Otherwise your ass would be in the damn hole so long, you wouldn't be recognizable. Now get your ass out in that hallway for mid-day count," he instructed him and pushed him towards the door.

Jayshawn walked towards the wall outside his cell with the rest of the inmates waiting on the guards to walk past for the midday count. The guards were taking their time, talking about what they had done over the weekend, and five minutes later, they were finished.

"In your cells!" one of the guards yelled as all the inmates began to make their way back to their cells.

Jayshawn laughed and walked back to his cot and picked up the mail that the guard had left on his bed. Jayshawn looked at the two letters that were sitting there. One was from his sister, and the other from Ariane. He had to admit, he had a little bit of love for her; for now. She'd held him down the entire time since he got caught and locked up. It amazed him, though, how naïve she was, because when he got arrested, she believed him when he told her that Alexis had hit on him and that he was innocent. He made sure to remain calm with her and tell her whatever she wanted to hear because he needed her to handle his business on the outside. Plus, she paid his attorney for him. He opened up her letter first, sat down on his cot and began to read.

Dear Jay,

I know it's been a minute since I came to see you. I'm sorry it's taking me so long to get back up that way but I got a new job to help take care of your legal fees and they are working me more than anticipated. By the time I get home I'm so tired and then my mom is riding my ass about dumb shit. I miss you like hell, baby. I can't wait for you to come home. Guess what? I got a surprise for you. But you can't get it until I come for a visit. I hope you're doing okay in there, baby. I hate that you aren't out here so that we can be together. Don't worry, though. You know I'm gonna hold it down. Mama said I was being stupid for waiting around on you but she don't know how much I love you. She told me that you're just using me. I just ignore her. I can't wait to move the hell out of her house, though. I put $200 on your books and I just gave your lawyer $300 he asked for. I will see you this weekend, baby. I love you.

Ariane

Jayshawn put the letter back in the envelope and smirked. *Damn, this girl makes things so easy*, he thought to himself.

He knew he had done some fucked up stuff to Ariane but she kept coming back. *Oh well,* he thought. *If she wanna be stupid, let her.* He wrote her a letter back to let her know that it was fine for her to come for a weekend visit. He wanted to make sure he kept her happy for as long as he was in there so that she could eventually get him out and he could tie up some loose ends.

He picked up the second letter from his sister. He knew she wasn't too happy to hear from him but, that was still his family.

J,

I don't know what else to say to get you to understand the amount of damage you done. I got your letter telling me what you think I should know. But I'm not stupid. I'm not one of these bitches that you are out here fucking. You can't just feed me some bullshit and expect me to believe it. You tried to kill my best friend and because of that, I don't think she and I will ever be close again because of the stupid shit you did. It's bad enough that you had to fuckin kidnap someone and then you and that dumb ass bitch try to kill her, but my best friend? You're supposed to be my brother. I looked out for you and fucked with you when no one else would. And this is how you repay me? Well, fuck you. Don't bother writing back because I will return to sender if I see anything else from you. You need to seek fucking help. Stay the hell away from me, and stay the hell away from Alexis. I hope they put your ass under the jail you bastard. You're sick in the fuckin head and I can't believe I'm related to your bitch ass. You're dead to me. If you ever get out, and I pray that you don't because you are a psychopath, please leave me and my family alone. We've been through enough. This will be my only letter to you.

Tamika

Jayshawn balled the letter up and threw it in the trash. He punched the wall over and over because he was so angry. He paced the floor of his small cell, not even noticing that his knuckles were bleeding. A guard walked past as Jayshawn was punching the walls and yelled to him.

"Hey! Inmate! Cut that shit out! Ain't no point in you tryna plead insanity now, you fuck!" Officer Morrison yelled to him laughing.

"Fuck you!" Jayshawn spat at him.

The guard stopped laughing and walked up to Jayshawn. "What did you say to me, you muthafucker?"

Jayshawn jumped at the cell. "You heard me, you monkey muthafucka! Fuck you! Fuck you and fuck this shit. I ain't scared like the rest of these bitches," he yelled.

The other inmates around Jayshawn's cell watched in amazement. It was so quiet, it was almost as if they were in a movie theater.

Officer Morrison was pissed and all you could hear was the mumbles of fear and amusement from the other inmates. The guard got his key out to open the cell. "That's it, asshole. Since you wanna show off for your friends, how about you spend a week in a cell by yourself? Let's go!!!" The guard grabbed Jayshawn by his collar and dragged him out the door.

"Get off me, muthafucka! Let me go! You ain't shit, bitch!" you could hear Jayshawn screaming down the hall. All the inmates just looked on in awe and started cheering for their fellow inmate. The stunt Jayshawn just pulled was going to make him legendary.

The guard got to the solitary cell and threw Jayshawn in. He didn't hesitate to take his night stick and hit Jayshawn in the back of his legs to make him fall. Jayshawn had challenged him in front of inmates and at Hoke Correctional Institution, it was either kill or be killed. The minute an inmate thought they could take a guard, it was a wrap. The state's budget had the prisons overcrowded and placing maximum security inmates in a minimum security facility. The guard made sure to make his authority known and was one of the most hated in all the years he worked there. He struck Jayshawn once more in the back to make sure he got the hint.

"Aaaahh!" Jayshawn screamed out as he grabbed his back.

"Shut the fuck up!" the guard yelled as he slammed the door shut, leaving Jayshawn alone for a week.

Jayshawn lay there and groaned in pain for a few minutes before trying to get up. As he sat up, the lights in his cell went out. He looked and saw all the other lights on and mumbled under his breath. He knew the guard did it on purpose. He sat in the dark and vowed that the guard would get his.

*

Alexis woke up in a cold sweat. She looked around only to realize she was in her bedroom. Chub Chub sat at the foot of her bed and sat up, staring at her as she collected her thoughts. She looked over at the other side of her bed to see Collin wasn't in the bed. She picked up her cell phone and saw that it was 5:13am. She figured he was out for his morning run. Knowing she wouldn't be able to go back to sleep, she figured she would get her day started a little earlier.

She got out of her bed and walked into her bathroom, cutting on her shower. Chub Chub was hot on her heels, as always. She petted him and walked to the kitchen.

"Come on, greedy. Let's get you something to eat," she told him.

She smiled as her dog's ears perked up at the sound of eating. Sometimes she swore he was human. She poured his dog food in his bowl as he wagged his tail vigorously. She filled his water dish then went to the hot shower that awaited her. She walked into her room and Waka Flocka's "No Hands" played loudly. Alexis jumped at the sudden noise then frowned as she walked over to her phone. The caller ID displayed "Unknown" and Alexis ignored it. Undressing, she got into the shower.

A few minutes later, she heard her phone ringing again. She got out the shower to catch the phone. "Hello?" she answered.

"Click," was all she heard from the phone line disconnecting. She carried the phone with her to the bathroom, placing it on the bathroom windowsill and getting back in the shower. Moments later, she heard her phone again. She pulled her shower curtain back to see that her phone displayed an unidentified caller again. She pushed the end button on her phone to send the call to voicemail. No sooner had she closed the shower curtain to finish her shower, her phone rang again.

"Aaaah!" she screamed out in frustration. She picked up the phone mad as hell. "Hello?" she screamed. She could hear someone breathing on the other end of the phone. "I can hear you breathing on the phone. What the hell do you want?! Say something!" Alexis screamed.

"Um, don't hang up," the voice said.

"Who the fuck is this?" Alexis asked.

"It's Tamika," she answered anxious.

Alexis stopped and cut the shower off. "Why are you calling me? What do you want? You think it's funny to be calling my phone all day and hanging up? Huh?"

Tamika was confused. "Lex, I- I don't know what you're talking about. I haven't called you at all. This is the first time I have called you," she said.

"Bullshit. I have over six calls today from an unknown number. So miss me with that. Now I'm going to ask you one more time. What do you want?!" Alexis said angrily.

"Look, Lex, I know you're mad at me. But I just really need you to know that I didn't know anything about it, I swear. I was just as surprised as everyone else. I didn't know that he was capable of some shit like that Lex. Really," Tamika apologized, crying into the phone.

Alexis listened to Tamika crying. She seemed like she was sincere in her words but Alexis wasn't ready to believe it yet. "Look, Tamika, all I know is that I can't trust you. I can't trust no fuckin' body. Your brother and his fucking psycho ass girlfriend damn near fucking killed me and you didn't say shit when everything was found out. You didn't pick up the phone not one time and call or nothing. On top of that, your dyke ass tried to fuck me when you knew I don't get down that way!" Alexis was yelling into the phone, trying not to cry.

"Lex, listen–"

"No, you listen!" Alexis continued. "I done been through more fucking shit than I can handle in the last year. I don't have time for this. Don't fucking call me again!" she screamed into the phone before hanging up.

Alexis walked into her bedroom and threw the phone down on the bed. She sat down on the edge and thought about her ex-friend and everything she had been through. She curled up on her bed and let the tears fall drifting off to sleep.

Alexis woke a few hours later to a dark room. *Did I cut that light out*, she asked herself. Quietly, she opened the drawer of her nightstand and pulled out her Ruger 9 millimeter. Taking the safety off, she got out her bed and threw on her sweat suit that sat in the chair she kept there just in case. She could see that there was a light on in the front of the house. She opted to call out, thinking it was Collin, but changed her mind. *Hell nah, I ain't bout to do that shit. I ain't some dumb blonde white girl*, she thought to herself. She slid out the cracked bedroom door with her gun cocked. It was almost as if she was in a scene of *Criminal Minds* the way she moved quietly in the house. She saw the large shadow on the wall and pointed her gun.

"If you move, I will blow your fucking brains out all over this fucking floor!" Alexis said. Getting closer, she realized it was

Collin. "Damn it, babe, why the fuck didn't you let me know you were going to be here?" she asked.

Collin stood frozen with his keys in his hand. "Whoa. Okay, Lex. What the hell is up with you? Why the fuck you pulling out your damn piece?"

Alexis stood in front of him, angry. "Why'd I pull my piece? Are you serious? Because you scared the fuck out of me, Collin, that's why!" she told him. "I thought someone had broken into the house."

Collin walked over to Alexis and took the gun away from her. "Babe, you need to calm down. Everything is okay. I got you. Aight, ma?"

Alexis shook her head as if she understood and hugged him tight. Collin could sense something was up.

"Hey, what's the deal, bae? You have never been this jumpy before," he told her.

Alexis tried to talk as she felt the tears. "I don't know. It's just like everything has been getting to me today and I don't know why," she cried. "I was at Dr. Rhimes' office today and I guess I started thinking about everything that happened. And then on top of that, Tamika's ass called me today."

Collin looked surprised at that one. "Word? How'd that go?"

Alexis sighed. "Not good. Like all she kept saying was that she didn't know and she wanted me to forgive her but I'm like, you fuckin got a brother that damn near killed me, AND you fucking tried to get at me on the low. Why the fuck do I want to have that shit in my life right now?" She was screaming at this point.

"Okay, well, I need you to calm the hell down though, for real. Like you screaming at me ain't gonna fix the situation. Sit down," he instructed her.

Alexis walked over towards her couch and sat down. She cut the TV on simply because it was too quiet but she wasn't really paying it any attention. Collin took the gun and walked into her bedroom to put it back in her drawer. He walked back in and sat down next to her on the couch.

"Now look, babe, I know that this has been real hard for you. And I'm not even going to lie and say I know what it feels like. But I think you need to talk to your girl. She didn't do anything and from what you have told me about her. Y'all have been friends way too long for you to do her dirty like that," he told her.

Alexis looked at him, surprised. She heard him but she wasn't sure if she should give in. She let her defenses get the better of her. "I mean damn, Collin. Really? You taking up for her like you fuckin the bitch or something."

Collin backed up and looked at her like she was insane. "You have got to be kidding me. So, because you're pissed off because of your own damn dumb ass decisions and actions lately, you wanna get mad at me and accuse me of fucking a girl who I've never even met? Wow, you really are on some bullshit Lex," he said.

"Wait a minute, wait a minute. What the fuck you mean, dumb ass decision and actions? Right now the only dumb ass decision and action that I'm seeing is being with your trifling, inconsiderate ass," Alexis said, regretting it the minute it came out of her mouth. She knew she needed to apologize but, her pride wouldn't let her do it.

Collin stifled a laugh and walked over to the coat rack picking up his line jacket. "You know what? You right. So I'm gonna take my inconsiderate ass and go the fuck home. I ain't got time for this shit," he said. He grabbed his keys and walked out, slamming the door behind him.

Alexis stood and let out a yell of frustration. She picked up her phone and called him to tell him to come back but it went straight to voicemail. Angry at herself, she put the alarm on and went to bed.

*

2003

"Shawn, we gotta get rid of this bitch, and quick. Too many people are starting to snoop around and I'm tired of looking at her, and damn sure fucking tired of you staring at her ass all the time," Keisha said while Jayshawn sat on his bed smoking a blunt.

It seemed like that's all he had been doing the last few days was smoking and making comments on Alexis. Keisha was pissed because he was too fascinated with her. *First Henderson, now this bitch*, she thought to herself. *But this will all be over soon. Because if this nigga don't get his shit together, it's a wrap*, she told herself.

"Chill," Jayshawn said in between puffs. "Ain't nobody fucking coming around like that. That shit's all in your mind." He leaned back and closed his eyes, relaxing to let the weed hit his system.

"Shawn, where the fuck you been? Nigga, it was just two cops at her fucking apartment! They been questioning the neighbors and shit. Hell, I'm surprised they haven't started checking apartments in the area! We done had this bitch here for fuckin' five days Shawn. Enough is enough. Let's just get rid of her and follow the plan," Keisha ranted.

Jayshawn put his blunt out and sat it on his dresser. "Damn, babe," he said softly. "You had a lot on your mind, huh? Come here," he told her.

Hesitant, Keisha walked to him by his bed. Jayshawn grabbed her by her throat before she could blink. She tried to pry his fingers off of her, but he only squeezed tighter.

"I'm getting real sick of your smart ass mouth. You do what the fuck I say. You hear me, bitch?" Jayshawn asked through his gritted teeth.

Unable to speak, Keisha shook her head yes.

"Good. Now get your ass up and go get me some Swishers."

Keisha stood up once he released her neck, coughing and gasping for air. She walked out the room and left quickly. Jayshawn heard the door close and walked over to the closet. He opened it to see Alexis huddled in the corner, bound at the feet and hands with the electrical tape on her mouth. She tried to push herself further into the corner but Jayshawn began to pull her out. She cried 'no' through the tape, but they went unanswered. Jayshawn untied her hands and feet and walked her to the bathroom.

"If you try anything, I will fucking kill you," he threatened her as he cut on the shower.

She was grateful he was letting her bathe because she had gone five days with no shower.

"Get in the shower," he told her.

She stepped in and looked around to see if there was anything that she could use to fight him off.

"Don't even think about it," He told, her realizing what she was doing.

She stood in the water as he lathered her body up and washed her. Alexis' eyes grew large as she saw Jayshawn picking up a razor. He began to shave her as he cleaned. Alexis stood scared, not knowing what he would do. She felt his fingers enter her and she tried to fight.

He picked her up and dragged her to his bed, threw her down and quickly unzipping his pants. He entered her quickly, pushing harder and harder with every thrust. He quickened his pace and Alexis lay in silence as the tears streamed down her face. She was dry and raw from the attack and every thrust was as painful as the one before.

Ten minutes later, he finished and dressed her in some of his old clothes, tied her with rope and stuck her back in the closet. Alexis heard the front door open and Jayshawn had a smirk on his face as he closed the door shut.

"Not a moment too soon," he said, smiling.

Alexis sat in the dark closet and prayed for God to end her life.

*

Alexis woke up in the dark closet to yelling and glass breaking. She cringed at the sound of Jayshawn's voice booming through the apartment at Keisha. She knew they were arguing about her. Keisha made it clear that she didn't want Alexis alive at all. She heard Keisha scream a few seconds before a loud bump. The voices got closer and she could tell that he was bringing her into the bedroom.

"Shut the fuck up, bitch, and get your ass in here!" Jayshawn slapped her so hard that she fell to the floor.

"Shawn, please!" Keisha begged. "I'm sorry."

She tried to get up, but Jayshawn just kicked her, knocking her back down. Before she knew what was happening, he was sitting on her with his hands around her throat. He gripped harder and harder and Keisha began to feel herself slipping from consciousness. She tried to grab his hands and pry them off her, unsuccessfully.

Boom! Boom! Boom!

Jayshawn stopped when he heard someone banging at the door. He let her go and walked out the room towards the front door. He looked out the peephole and saw Ariane standing there with her arms folded across her chest. She knocked hard again.

"Open up the door, Jayshawn. I know you're in there with some bitch because I could hear you yelling when I pulled up. Open up the damn door!" she said as she continuously banged on the door.

Jayshawn yanked the door open, scaring Ariane. "Have you lost your fucking mind bitch? You don't come popping up at my muthafucking house!" he yelled at her. *What the fuck is wrong with these stupid ass bitches?* he thought to himself.

"Why you not answering your phone, Jayshawn? I been calling you all fucking day! And who the fuck is in the house? I know I heard a bitch, Jayshawn. Who the fuck is she?!" Ariane yelled.

Jayshawn looked at her like she was crazy and wanted to choke her out right there at his front door. He stepped outside and closed his door when he noticed police entering the complex.

"Get your ass in here," he told her, against his better judgment. He knew the minute she got inside, she was going to start crying and whining about Keisha but he needed to be out of the cops' view. He pulled her in the apartment, quickly closing the door behind him.

"Why you pulling me so hard? Get off me!" Ariane demanded.

"Damn, will you just shut up?" Jayshawn said. "All I been dealing with is nagging and bullshit. I ain't time for this shit. Just sit down and shut up," he told her.

Keisha came walking from the bedroom and Ariane jumped up. "Oh, you wanna go off on me but this bitch is in your fucking house? Who the fuck are you?" she asked.

Keisha walked up on her and punched her in the face, sending Ariane flying onto the floor. "Bitch, don't worry about who the fuck I am!"

Jayshawn sat back, shocked at what had just happened. *Damn*, he thought.

He continued to watch as Ariane tried to regain her balance and defend herself against Keisha. She squared up and swung but missed, allowing Keisha to hit her with a low punch to her stomach. She fell into the wall, denting it from the force. Jayshawn's dick was starting to get hard from watching Keisha attack her. He pulled Keisha off after a few more minutes.

"Aight, baby, calm down. Go in the room and let me get rid of this bitch. You made daddy excited and I gotta work some of this shit off." He moved her towards the back room and smacked her on the ass. "Go on back there and roll daddy one."

Keisha walked in the back room smirking and closed the door.

Jayshawn walked over to a damn near unconscious Ariane, yanking her up off the floor. "Uh huh, you came over here talking all that shit and acting all big and bad and look at you. Get your ass up." He pushed her towards the door and shoved her out. Ariane was groggy and crying from the pain Keisha gave her.

"I'm sorry," she told Jayshawn. "Please, don't do this. Please!"

Jayshawn slammed the door shut in her face, leaving her standing there.

Ariane stood there registering what had just happened. She could barely see out of her left eye because Keisha hit her so hard. She thought about knocking on the door again until another thought came to mind. *Oh, I'll fix you, bitch*, she thought to herself. *Fucked my nigga? You're done, hoe.* She walked to her car and pulled out her cell phone as she got in. Dialing the number, she got ready for the performance of a lifetime.

"911, what's your emergency?" the operator said.

"Yes, I need to report an assault," Ariane cried, smiling on the outside.

*

CHAPTER THREE

Alexis drove through downtown Greensboro on her way to campus. She rolled the windows down to let the cool spring breeze in. She almost didn't go to class because she was up late thinking about everything that had happened. She spent almost an hour texting a bunch of her friends until she finally passed out. She woke up dragging when her alarm clock went off the next morning.

She was driving down Elm Street and decided to stop at the new Subway to grab a breakfast sandwich since she had almost an hour before class. She parked her car at the curb and put money into the meter. Her phone buzzed as she walked down the sidewalk. She pulled her phone out and almost tripped when she read the name.

Henderson: Hey, wassup, you messaged me?

Alexis, now closer to the restaurant, was taken by surprise; unsure if she should respond. While in the midst of texting her friends last night, she had sent him a text by mistake but she didn't expect him to respond. The last time she talked to him, he was breaking it off with her and moving to Virginia for a job. She couldn't believe that he was leaving her. He was right by her side after she was rescued from Jayshawn and Keisha's captivity. He never left her alone and showed her a whole new side to him during all the nights that she cried from fear she would be taken again.

Alexis walked into the restaurant and waited in line to order her food. She decided to respond to his message.

Alexis: Sorry I was messaging some of my friends last night and I accidentally messaged you. My apologies.

She put her phone back in her bag and walked up to order her food. The associate prepared her breakfast sandwich and she walked to the checkout counter to pay for her food. She felt her phone vibrate again. Pulling her wallet out of her purse, she glanced at the phone, seeing that Henderson had responded. She decided to talk and see what he was up to.

Henderson: You good. I figured it was an accident as late as it was.

Alexis smiled at the thought of him looking at his phone half-sleep. She grabbed her food and headed out the door back to her car.

Alexis: Glad you understand. How have you been?

Henderson: I'm good. Chillin. Workin. You?

Alexis: About the same. Tryna hurry up and graduate. I applied for grad school in Atlanta. How's the new job going?

Henderson: That's wassup. Which school you apply to? The job is going ok for what it is. Plenty of clients to keep you busy. But shit, it pays the bills.

Alexis: I definitely feel you on that. And how is the diva herself?

Henderson: Man, she wearing me out. Her ass got my ma doing any and everything that she ask for. Smh.

Alexis: Like you didn't have anything to do with it!

Alexis was in her car with the radio playing and still in park. She put her car in drive and began driving to campus. She put her Bluetooth in and decided to call after seeing a county sheriff in the lane next to her, and she definitely was not trying to get a ticket. Henderson picked up on the second ring.

"I'm glad I'm not doing anything important right now. You know, some of us do have jobs," he joked.

"Very funny. I'm driving and it's a sheriff next to me and if I get another ticket, my father is threatening to take my car away. And we both know I am not giving that up," she replied.

"And we both know I'm not giving that up," he mocked. "Okay, daddy's girl. I forgot your ass is spoiled," he reminded her sarcastically.

Alexis rolled her eyes as she neared her campus. "And I forgot how much of an asshole you can be," she sighed.

"Well, you the one that called this asshole," he reminded her.

"Uh huh. That's because it was either call you or get a ticket. At this point, sir, a ticket don't sound half-bad," she joked.

"Yea, okay. So what's good?" he asked.

"Nothing much, on my way to class. Just left from getting some breakfast," she told him.

"Okay, let me rephrase the question. When I say what's good, I mean what's up. Like why did you call me at two in the morning?" he inquired.

Alexis feigned surprise. "Oh. I just had some stuff on my mind, and I figured you would be one of the few people that would understand; so, I thought I would hit you up. I honestly wasn't thinking about the time when I did so, my bad about that," she replied apologetic.

"You good," he told her. He got serious for a minute. "So what's going on? You good? What happened?"

Alexis sighed heavily. "Man, everything. The last few days have been really crazy. Like, I keep having these crazy ass dreams about that shit. And I'm trying Hen to handle it, but this shit came out of nowhere. I feel paranoid all the time, I hardly sleep, and nothing seems to be going right. I'm just ready to graduate so I can get the hell out of here," she let out.

"Damn. You still tryna head to Atlanta for grad school?" he asked her.

"Yea," she answered, perking up. "I think it'll be a good thing for me to just get away. And I mean, my grandmother is there, and after graduation, it's not like I will really have anything to keep me here," she said, fishing.

"Oh, word?" he responded. "So what does your…boyfriend gotta say about that?" he asked.

Alexis was irritated by the way he said that. "Why you gotta say it like that?" she asked with an attitude.

"I didn't mean nothing by it, baby," he told her smoothly.

"I'm not your baby," she snapped.

Henderson stifled a laugh. "The minute I made you explode, you were mine; so it don't matter what you say."

Alexis' pussy immediately got wet. She could feel her body shudder as she pulled into the parking lot of the campus. She tried not to think about the spark that he just lit in her panties but, he was making it difficult.

"Anyway," she said, trying to change the subject. "Shouldn't you be doing some work?"

"Oh, I'm working. Don't worry about that. Where your man at?" he asked.

"What man?" Alexis said smugly.

"Oh, another one bites the dust, huh?" he said.

"I mean, we're just…I don't even know what we are, but I just can't deal with someone that can't understand everything that I been through," she replied hesitantly.

"So what happened with that? Y'all been kicking it for a minute," he asked.

"Last night this nigga came over and I was actually asleep. So when I woke up and saw the light on, I grabbed my piece out of the drawer in the nightstand and ran up in the living room. So when that calms down, we get into an argument over Tamika's stupid ass," she responded, practically yelling.

"I thought you and Tamika wasn't cool?" Henderson asked, confused.

"We not!" Alexis answered quickly. "This bitch fucking called my phone all day long yesterday and kept fucking hanging up and shit. So the last time she called, I called her ass out and she was tryna apologize and shit. But I didn't wanna hear it cause it's just too much damage that's been done. So I hung up on her. I told Collin all that but he was just saying that I was overreacting and that I need to talk to her. But I'm not tryna deal with that shit." She was practically crying as she explained everything to him.

"Damn. Yea, that's fucked up. I mean, I think ole boy is right. But I know your hardheaded ass ain't gonna do shit unless you wanna do it, so I all I can say is just take your time," he told her.

Alexis smiled sitting in her car. That was one thing that she loved about Henderson. He didn't push her to do anything. He let her fall on her ass and then said his piece.

"Yea, I know. I'm good. She can go her way and I will go mine," Alexis told him.

"Come see me," Henderson said suddenly.

Alexis was caught off guard. "I'm sorry, what?" she asked.

"I said come see me. Come to VA and chill for the weekend. It ain't like you got shit else to do," he told her. "That way you can get your mind off the dumb shit and just chill for a while," he suggested.

Alexis didn't know what to say. "Well damn, that was sudden," she joked. "What brought this on?"

"I just told you," he said bluntly. "So you coming or what?"

Alexis laughed. "Well, I guess so. But I don't get out of class until four and then I have a therapy session," she told him.

"Ok, so what? Do what you need to do and get your ass on the road. I'll text you the address in a few," he said.

"Alright. Well, I guess I will see you in a bit then. You sure about this?" she asked just to be sure. She didn't want him inviting her just out of pity.

"What did I say?" he asked her, annoyed.

"Okay, okay. I will be there. But let me go ahead and go because I have been sitting in this parking lot for like the past ten minutes talking to you and I gotta get to class so I am not late," she informed him.

"Aight, cool," he told her. "Just hit me up."

Alexis found herself smiling again. "Bye," she said, disconnecting her call.

Alexis put her phone in her purse and opened her glove box to get her student parking pass. The campus had been cracking down on students parking without passes and the last thing that Alexis wanted was for them to tow her car.

Her father got her a brand new midnight black Mercedes C230 and she loved it. Her windows were tinted and she had a keyless entry as well as automatic starter. After she convinced her father to let her stay in North Carolina to finish school, he insisted that she not only move into a safer and much more gated community, but he got a new car for her as well. She loved the car not just because it was sporty, but it had everything she needed just in case she had to get away quick.

She reached over to close her glove box and grab her purse and book bag to begin heading to class. She closed her door, hit the alarm key and smiled. She hadn't seen Henderson in almost a year since he graduated so she smiled at the thought of the great weekend she was going to have.

*

Ariane ducked down as Alexis walked past her. She waited until Alexis was halfway down the hill before she sat up. She had been sitting in the car for the last twenty minutes. Not sure what she was doing, Ariane just sat and watched. She was able to easily follow Alexis from the restaurant to campus. She could tell that she was distracted. She didn't mind waiting in the car though. She was able to write Jayshawn a letter while periodically checking to see what Alexis was doing. She decided to finish her letter before she put the next part of her plan into action. She figured it would give her time to calm her nerves and relax since the baby had her up all night.

Dear Jayshawn,

Damn, baby, I miss you so much. I hope that you are holding it together. I know it's been a lot going on out here that I can't wait to tell you about. I tried to come visit you a few days ago but they wouldn't even let me past the front gate. They said something about you being in solitary confinement. What happened? Is everything ok? Baby, you gotta be careful while you're in there. Please try not to get into trouble. They told me that I could call up there in a week to see if I could get put back on your visitors list. I really hope I can because I have some really good news and baby, some news just needs to be said in person. I know I have said it a thousand times before but, baby, I am so sorry for everything that happened. I was so angry that you were messing with that girl that I never thought they would be tryna set you up. I blame myself every day for not believing you and you having to deal with all of this. But don't worry, baby, I'm going to fix it. No worries, my love, we will be together again soon. I can't wait to get a letter back from you! Anytime I see an envelope with your name I get excited. Well, baby, I have to go. I have to take care of some business (I will tell you about that later, too). I love you.

I'm going to put some more money on your books too so you can get whatever you need in there. See you soon. Don't forget to add my name back to your visitation list!

Love,

Ariane

She folded the letter, placing it in an envelope and labeling it with the inmate information required. She looked at her dashboard and saw the clock displayed 10:38am. She needed to make it to the engineering building by 10:50, and with the way she was moving the last few days, she needed to get moving fast. She rubbed her stomach as she opened the door.

"Ok, peanut; now you may feel a little shaken in a few minutes but don't worry. Everything is going to be okay. I gotta do this so that way me, you and daddy can be a family. So just trust mommy. This should be quick." Ariane grabbed her things and began to walk down the hill towards the engineering building.

Ten minutes later, Ariane made it to the building. She would have made it sooner, however, she stopped twice to catch her breath and rest. Her back was wet with sweat from walking and she was huffing and puffing by the time she reached the building. She looked at her watch and saw that she had a few minutes. She had learned Collin's schedule a few weeks before and knew he would be in the building until 10:55am when his class ended. Her plan was to accidentally bump into him and get his help. That was the hardest part. The rest would be easy.

She walked into the building and took the elevator to the second floor. She made sure that the hallways were empty. She walked over to the ladies restroom. She walked inside to make sure it was empty. Satisfied, she checked all the stalls and walked out.

Doing another quick scan of the hallway, Ariane pulled the fire alarm, causing the hallways to flood with students and professors within seconds. She ducked around the corner towards the restroom and waited.

Ariane had planned to just get rid of Collin when he left Alexis house, but that would be too risky. The idea came to her when she was reading one of Jayshawn's old letters. She began watching Collin to learn his routine and schedules, and actually felt sorry for him. *It's too bad*, she thought to herself. *You seem like such a good dude. You just fucking got with the wrong bitch.* She watched all of the students evacuating and stepped out, ready to put on the performance of a lifetime.

*

Collin was sitting in class when he heard the fire alarm go off. The students looked around at each other for a few seconds waiting for a reaction from the professor. When he saw the look of surprise on his professor's face, Collin decided this was not a drill and grabbed his belongings.

"Okay, students, let's exit the room, please; quickly and safely. Please, no running," Professor Martin instructed.

The professor's words went unheard as students ran quickly down the halls to attempt to get out of the building as soon as possible. Collin looked to see if his fraternity brother was still in the classroom.

"Aye yo, Will, let's go!" Collin yelled to his brother. Will ran alongside him as they tried to head to the doors with the numerous other students in the building not wanting to risk their lives. Doors were being opened and the students were running out in hordes. Collin and his brother were headed down the steps when Collin saw a pregnant girl headed in their direction. She had tears on her face. Something told Collin to keep going but she looked scared.

"Will, go ahead. I'll be down in a second," Collin told him. He saw his bother hesitate but he went ahead.

Collin ran over to the girl. "Hey, are you okay?" he asked her.

The girl looked up at him and her face was stained with tears. "No. I....I think I might be in labor, and I can't find my keys anywhere," she told him.

Collin frowned at the girl's bad timing. "Okay, well, calm down. First thing we need to do is get you out of this building and then get you an ambulance," he told her as he pulled his cell phone out of his pocket.

A look of panic came over her face. She was not prepared for that answer. "No!" she said quickly. "I...I can't afford that $500 they charge for ambulance rides," she lied.

Collin began walking her to the stairs. "Okay, well, we have got to get out of here so we can worry about everything else when we get out there. Now, so that we can get out of here quick, the best thing for me to do is pick you up and carry you down the stairs, okay?" he asked her as he prepared himself to pick her up. He quickly sized her up and determined that even pregnant, she was maybe 130 pounds. The girl shook her head yes and he picked her up, carrying her down the stairs.

He walked out of the building carrying her as far away from it as possible. At this point, there were several first responders from firefighters, to emergency medical technicians to assist if there were any injuries. Firefighters went into the building to make sure that it was completely evacuated. Collin placed Ariane down.

"Ok, I'm going to go get one of the EMT's and bring them over here to look at you," He told her.

Ariane jumped quickly. "No, no, no! I think everything is okay. I think it was just the adrenaline from everything. Don't worry, I will be okay."

"Are you sure?" he asked. "I really think you should be looked at."

"Yea, I'm fine," she reassured him. "I just need to go lay down for a bit more now than anything."

"Okay, well, where did you park? I can walk you to your car," Collin suggested.

Ariane let out a dramatic sigh. "I lost my keys somewhere in the building."

Collin felt his phone vibrating in his pocket. He pulled it out to see his frat brother Will was calling.

"Hey, bro. I'm good. I'm over here by the bookstore. The girl I was helping lost her keys and I was just trying to make sure she was out. You good?" he asked.

His brother told him where he was and that he was ok.

"Okay, well, I'm going to take her to the hospital and I will meet up with you in a few," he told his brother. "Aight, bruh." He hung up the phone and put it back in his pocket.

Ariane stopped smirking just in time for Collin to turn back to her. "Okay, so I don't feel comfortable leaving you out here so this is what I'm going to do. I'm going to take you to the hospital where you can be seen medically. No arguments. Now I parked a little ways from here so I am going to go get the car and try to see if I can bring it as close as possible," he told her sternly.

Ariane looked around to see all of the fire trucks blocking many of the entrances to the building. "Uh, I don't think that is possible. I can walk; it's okay. Besides, they say that walking is good when you are in labor. It helps the contractions slow down. Besides, you've done enough for me as is. I don't mind," she assured him.

Hesitant, Collin agreed. He helped her up and began the walk to his car, making sure to stick close so that she wouldn't hurt herself. After a five minute walk, they reached his car. He opened the passenger door and helped her into the car. He walked over to the other side and started the car and pulled out to take her to the hospital.

"So, uh…are you having a boy or a girl?" he asked her to end the silence.

Ariane smiled. "I don't know. I wanted it to be a surprise," she said.

"Oh ok. That's cool. I know you and the dad must be excited," he told her.

She showed a genuine look of sadness for a moment as she placed her hands on her stomach. "Actually, he's not around. He left shortly after I found out. Said he wasn't ready for a baby. Haven't heard from him since," she lied as she worked up some tears.

Collin swallowed hard at the insensitive comment that he'd made. "I'm sorry. I didn't mean to make you upset. Hey, don't worry. I'm sure that baby will be happy either way."

"Thanks," she responded. "Hey, um, I hope I'm not being too much of an imposition. But, do you think you can take me home instead of to the hospital? The contractions have actually stopped so, I should be fine long enough to grab my hospital bag. It's got everything I need in there and I would feel better prepared with heading to the hospital. And I will call a cab to take me to the hospital. No worries," she persuaded him.

"I don't know. I mean, I don't want you to get home and then the contractions start back up again or something. Look, I know you don't know me like that but, I wouldn't feel comfortable doing that," Collin said, concerned.

Damn what a fucking choir boy! she thought to herself. He was making it difficult for her. Then she had an idea. "Ok, well, I understand. Tell you what. My house is actually closer than the hospital. I stay in an apartment complex off Wendover Avenue. You can take this exit and we will be there in about five or six minutes. You can wait there if you'd like until the cab comes, Mr. Superhero," she suggested.

Collin chuckled at the name she called him. "That's fine. And you don't need to worry about taking a cab. I can take you."

"Are you sure?" she asked sweetly.

"Yea, it's straight. Do you have anybody that you can call that can meet you at the hospital?" he asked her.

"Yea. I have a friend of mine from school. I think she's still in class right now, but I will text her and tell her to meet me there just in case. By the way, my name is Alicia," she said.

"Oh ok. I'm Collin," he introduced himself.

"So Collin, what are you; like a modern day superhero?" she asked with a laugh.

"Why you say that?" he asked, turning onto the next street.

"I mean, you were kind of like Clark Kent. Like you came out of nowhere. And then the next thing I know, you're picking me up and carrying me down the steps like some superhero in a movie," she joked.

Collin let out a laugh. "Nah, not a superhero. Just didn't want to leave you up there like that in that building. What I look like running past a pregnant woman and you could've been hurt?" he asked nicely.

Damn, he's kinda nice, Ariane thought. She just knew this was the kind of guy her mom always wanted her to date. But she had always been attracted to the bad boys. She attracted them like magnets. For a split second, she felt a twinge of guilt for dragging him into it. Then she remembered Jayshawn being locked up in prison and how she was going through this pregnancy alone.

"Um, where am I going?" Collin interrupted her thoughts.

"Oh! I'm sorry," she told him. "Make a left at this stop sign and the complex will be on the left," she instructed.

Collin followed the instructions and entered her complex. She gave him instructions on how to get to her building. He pulled up to the building and she opened the passenger door.

74

"Hey, do you mind walking with me inside so I can grab my bag, Superman?" she asked nicely.

Collin smiled and answered "Sure."

The two walked to the apartment and entered. Ariane told him to take a seat and offered him something to drink. She went into the kitchen, took a few sodas out the refrigerator and poured them into the glasses. She needed to get him out of the room so she could slip the drugs into his drink.

"If you want, you can go and grab the bag out of my bedroom. It's sitting right by the door," she told him.

Without hesitation, he walked towards the back, giving her time to slip the drugs into his drink. She had been reading online and found some stuff from the pharmacy that her mother worked at that would help. Collin came back into the room and she walked out of the kitchen with the drinks in her hand.

"Here you go," she said as she handed him the glass. She had put enough in there to take down a small bear and was hoping he wouldn't taste it through the soda.

Collin accepted the drink and drank half the glass from thirst. "This tastes a little different. What kind of soda is this?" he asked her.

Ariane was panicking on the inside. "Oh, it's diet. I have to be careful of the amount of caffeine that I drink so I mostly drink diet," she lied quickly.

"Oh ok. Makes sense," he told her.

"Ouch!" Ariane screamed, feigning contractions to change the subject.

Collin jumped up. "Are you okay?" he asked her.

"Yea, I think I just had another contraction. I'll be fine, I just need to sit down for a second," she said as she pretended to walk slowly to the couch. He helped her sit down and sat next to her.

"Ok, give it a few minutes and then if there aren't any more contractions, we can go to the hospital, okay?" he asked her.

Ariane shook her head and smiled on the inside at how she got his mind off the drink. She knew soon it would be taking affect, so she stalled.

"Yea, that's fine. I'm gonna text my home girl and tell her to meet us there." She said as she looked up at him standing over her concerned. "Um, can you sit down? You're making my neck hurt on top of everything else," she joked.

Collin sat down and put his drink down. He wasn't sure what to do because the last time he saw anyone go into labor was in a video from sex education. His head was hurting and he was beginning to sweat from nerves. His heart was racing. He felt like his heart was about to leap out his chest. He felt himself getting dizzy. *What the hell?* he thought to himself. *Am I having a panic attack or something?*

Ariane looked over to see Collin's eyes getting very heavy. His body was wavering on the couch where he sat. "Are you okay?" she asked him. "Collin? Can you hear me?" she asked, faking concern.

Collin looked to see Ariane staring at him. It almost seemed as if she had a smirk on her face. Before he could ask, he blacked out.

*

"Class dismissed. Remember, there will be a study session in the library in the Bluford room tonight at 6pm for all those that need extra help for next week's exam," Professor Bradshaw said as students were preparing to leave.

Alexis stood up to gather her things and put her stuff in her bag. Her phone was going off in her purse but she'd ignored it the entire class. She tried not to look at her phone in her economics class because she really needed to focus and have no distractions. She was about to pull her phone out when she looked out the window and saw several fire trucks and police cars a few hundred yards ahead. One of her classmates Tanya looked with her.

"Dang, I wonder what happened," Alexis asked out loud.

"It was some type of fire in the engineering building," Tanya told her.

Alexis immediately began to worry because she knew Collin was in the building for class. Even though she hadn't talked to him, she was still worried. She grabbed her stuff and ran out the building to find him. She pulled her phone out her purse and called his phone as she sorted through the crowd of on looking students and faculty. The phone went straight to voicemail.

"Hey Collin, it's Lex. I saw that there was a fire so just call me to let me know you're ok? Please?" she messaged hanging up the phone.

Alexis saw a firefighter walking past her as she continued to look for Collin. "Excuse me," she said, stopping him. "Do you know if everyone is out of the building?"

The dark skinned firefighter looked at her as if he was in a hurry, and then relaxed. "They are checking all the floors now but they do believe that everyone is out of the building, ma'am," he informed her.

Alexis felt a little relief in knowing that Collin was safe. She took a second look at the firefighter. *Damn, he's fine as hell*, she thought to herself. "Thanks, Captain…Russell?" she said as she looked at his tag on his jacket.

The firefighter smiled a gorgeous smile. "Not a captain. Just a regular firefighter, ma'am," he told her.

"Well, again, thanks. I'm Alexis," she told him. She held out her hand for him to take it.

"Nice to meet you, Alexis. Jonathon Russell," he said. "Look, I know you're probably busy right now, so would I be wrong if I asked you for your number and I call you later when you have some time?" he asked, getting straight to the point.

Alexis had a look of surprise at his straight forward demeanor. "Well, you don't waste any time, do you?" she asked him. "Okay, 336-254-1327."

He stored the number in his phone. "Ok, I got you. I gotta go but, I will call you later," he said as he got ready to run back to his truck.

Alexis smiled and waved and walked off. She almost forgot what she was out there for until she saw Collin's frat brother.

"Will!" she called out. "Will!"

There was so much commotion that he didn't hear her. Alexis began walking uphill to her car and figured she would call him again in a few minutes. A few moments later, she spotted him but he wasn't alone. He was walking with a very pregnant young girl.

"What the hell?" she said as he watched him helping her into his car. "Oh, word? Clearly you ain't as upset as you let on, nigga," she spat.

She felt like a fool as she watched them drive off and every thought possible ran through her mind of how to hurt him. She knew she pissed him off but, she didn't expect him to be over her so fast. Remembering that Henderson had invited her to his place for the weekend, she smiled.

"I didn't need his ass anyway," she reassured herself. She got in her car and headed to her next class, fighting tears the whole way.

*

CHAPTER FOUR

Alexis stood in the elevator thinking about everything that happened throughout the day. She could barely focus in the rest of her classes because she was so mad at seeing Collin with that girl. She knew the girl from somewhere but she just couldn't place it. All she could think about was his smile as he helped her in the car. She was anticipating therapy today because she had a lot to get off her chest. The elevator stopped on the floor and she walked to his office.

Dr. Rhimes looked up to see Alexis walking through the door. "Good afternoon, Ms. Thomas. Take a seat. I'm going to go grab a coffee and then I will be right with you," he said as he walked down the hall.

Alexis took a seat and pulled her phone out to silence it. She looked down to see that she had a missed call from an unknown number. *This bitch just don't quit*, she thought to herself assuming Tamika was calling her again. She saw there was a voicemail and decided to ignore it. She cut her phone off and put it back in her bag. Dr. Rhimes walked in just as she was finishing.

"Well, how are we doing today?" he asked.

Alexis shook her head and let out a laugh. "You definitely asked the right question," she responded.

Dr. Rhimes put his glasses on and pulled out his notebook. "Sounds like you've had quite a day. Anything new that got you in this particular mood?" he inquired.

Alexis sat back in the chair and let out a loud sigh. "Everything just always seems to happen at one time," she said.

"Okay, so let's go one thing at a time," he suggested.

"Well, for starters, my boyfriend and I broke up," she told him. "He had come over last night and we got into an argument over my ex-best friend Tamika. She called me all day yesterday and I told her to leave me alone. He told me I was being childish and that she didn't do anything to me and that I should talk to her. I basically told him that who I chose to be friends with wasn't any of his business and that he needed to butt out. We kept going back and forth and I told him to get out and never come back," she said, now crying.

Dr. Rhimes reached over and handed her tissues to wipe her eyes. "It's ok. Take a few seconds and calm down. Now let's back up a bit and talk about Tamika. You said she contacted you several times yesterday?" he asked.

"Yes!" Alexis answered angrily. "She kept calling me from an unknown number but kept hanging up. Then she lied and said that she wasn't calling, but I know it was her!" she cried.

Dr. Rhimes, concerned, asked "Are you sure that it was Tamika that was contacting you continuously?"

"It had to be," Alexis said sniffling.

He looked at the pain on her face. "Alexis, why do you have so much resentment to Tamika? Is it because of what happened?" he asked.

Alexis got quiet and took a minute to respond. "She couldn't even say, 'I'm sorry,'" she whispered. "She sat there and saw me bleeding and walked away." Alexis broke down and let the tears flow as she remembered the night that she was found and the reaction Tamika had broken her heart.

"Alexis," Dr. Rhimes called her, interrupting her thoughts. "I want to take you back to the day that you were found. I'm going to use the process of hypnosis to help, okay?" he told her.

"Is it safe?" Alexis asked.

"Yes," Dr. Rhimes reassured her. "Just sit back and relax. Close your eyes and take a deep breath. Breathe deep and focus. Release all other thoughts."

Alexis leaned back and closed her eyes and began to relieve one of the most horrific days of her life.

*

2003

Alexis woke up in the dark closet scared. She heard the fight earlier with Ariane and Keisha. Alexis felt like she had been in the closet for weeks, and had lost track of how many days she had been there. *God, please*, she prayed, *I know that I haven't always done everything right. I know I have messed up in a lot of areas and knowingly did wrong. But is this my punishment? What did I do? Was my stepfather molesting me not enough? My being permanently messed up not enough? If this is how I'm going to go, just give me something. I don't want to die like this. I don't want to die in this damn closet. I deserve to live my life just as anybody else. I've been through enough, damn it! Please, God, don't let me die like this.*

Boom! Boom! Boom!

Alexis jumped to hear what sounded like someone banging on the door. She could hear Jayshawn telling Keisha to keep her quiet. Alexis closed her eyes and pretended as if she was asleep so as not to give Keisha any reason to hurt her. Keisha came into the room and opened the closet door. She snatched Alexis up by her hair and held a knife to her throat.

"If you make a sound, I will fucking cut your throat, bitch." Keisha threatened.

She moved Alexis to the bathroom and closed the door. She shoved Alexis in the bathtub and sat on the toilet seat, making sure to keep the knife close. On the outside, she was trying to be strong but she was panicking and scared. She didn't want to go to jail. Her leg began to shake as fear took over. Alexis lay in the tub and watched her break.

"Don't fucking look at me, bitch," Keisha whispered to her angrily. "I don't give a fuck what Jayshawn says. Your ass is dead tonight, bitch."

Alexis turned away. "Hell, I can drown your ass right here and now. It's as simple as you needed to bathe and the water just overflowed," Keisha said.

Alexis smirked with the tape in her mouth.

Keisha saw this and it angered her. "What the fuck is so funny?" she asked. She took the tape off of Alexis' mouth. "I said, what the fuck is so funny?"

Fuck it, Alexis thought to herself. *I'm tired of being scared.* "Oh, your man didn't tell you? He didn't tell you how he just brought me into this fucking bathroom and stripped my ass naked and put me in the shower, washing me? Huh? He didn't tell you that? Did he tell you that the reason he had to give me a bath is because he has been fucking me every chance he gets when you're not around?" Alexis let out a laugh. "You been trying so hard to get rid of me while your fuckin man has been fantasizing about me. So what? That's two niggas now that used to fuck you but had better fun fucking me? Henderson couldn't get enough of my ass. And Jayshawn went through all of this to get me. I mean, damn, it's gotta suck knowing your nigga has been fucking me and even took care of me. I bet if I promised him some more pussy he would kill you, huh?" she taunted.

Keisha was furious. She had suspected he was doing something with her, but hearing it come from Alexis' arrogant ass, she lost it. "You fuckin bitch!" she yelled as she jumped on Alexis. Angry, she dropped the knife and kept punching her over and over. "I'll kill you!" she yelled.

Alexis tried her best to fight her off with her hands bound. She covered her face to stop the blows. Keisha continued to punch harder and harder. Alexis saw the knife Keisha dropped on the floor next to the toilet. With all strength she had, she charged Keisha, knocking her to the floor, causing Keisha to be groggy. She grabbed the knife with her hands and rushed to cut herself free. She heard Keisha moaning behind her and hurried to get loose. She got the tape off as Keisha ran to attack her. Alexis turned around, knife in hand, and pushed it in hard into Keisha's stomach. Alexis pulled the knife out, stabbing her again. Keisha groaned in pain as she bled all over the bathroom floor.

Alexis grabbed the door handle of the bathroom and opened it quietly. She saw the closet door was open along with the bedroom door. She gripped the knife in her hand, preparing to protect herself if Jayshawn was on the other side. She tiptoed closer to the door and walked out in the living room.

"Freeze!"

Alexis turned around to see a police officer standing, gun aimed straight at her. Alexis froze and dropped the knife immediately. The adrenaline began to slow down and she felt herself getting lightheaded.

"My...my name is Alexis Thomas," she said. "I've been kidnapped." She fell out, losing consciousness.

*

Jayshawn and Keisha were sitting watching TV in the living room. Keisha was giving him head while he was smoking a blunt. Jayshawn leaned his head back as he took his hand and pushed Keisha's head further down on his dick. The TV was on low and the only sounds in the room were from the slurping from Keisha. After watching the fight between Ariane and Keisha, all he wanted to do was bend Keisha over and fuck her. He got off on stuff like that. Keisha was sucking him off like she was going for the gold in the Olympics. Jayshawn loved how her mouth felt on him. He took another hit of the blunt and blew the smoke out.

Boom! Boom! Boom!

Jayshawn jumped up as he heard banging on his door for the second time that day.

"I know this bitch didn't bring her ass back over here!" Keisha snapped at him.

Jayshawn pulled his pants up and walked over to the door ready to snap whoever's neck was at the door. He looked in the peephole and saw two police officers standing at the door. He turned to Keisha and motioned for her to be quiet.

Boom! Boom! Boom!

"Jayshawn Cheston! Police. Open up. We know you're in there," they yelled through the door.

Jayshawn looked to Keisha. "Get in the room and keep her quiet," he instructed.

Keisha shook her head and disappeared into the room. Jayshawn sprayed the living room to try to hide the smell of weed.

Boom! Boom! Boom!

"Last chance, Mr. Cheston. Open the door."

Jayshawn unlocked his door and opened it. "My bad, officers. I was in the room with my girl and you kind of caught us in the middle of something," he told the officers.

The officers looked at him with disdain. "Are you Jayshawn Cheston?" the officer asked him.

"Yea," Jayshawn answered.

The officers walked over to him and grabbed him, forcing his arms behind his back. One of the officers spoke, "We got a warrant for your arrest for the assault and battery of an Ariane Foster. She claims that you and another young lady assaulted her."

This fucking bitch called the cops! Jayshawn thought to himself. "Look officers, my girl and me been in the house all day. You can ask her," he told the cops.

The officer put the handcuffs on him and instructed his partner to go look in the bedroom for Keisha while he read him his rights, "You have the right to remain silent when questioned. Anything you say or do may be used against you in a court of law. You have the right to consult an attorney before speaking to the police and to have an attorney present during questioning now or in the future. If you cannot afford an attorney, one will be appointed for you before any questioning, if you wish. If you decide to answer any questions now, without an attorney present, you will still have the right to stop answering at any time until you talk to an attorney. Knowing and understanding your rights as I have explained them to you, are you willing to answer my questions without an attorney present?" the officer asked.

Jayshawn stood there quiet. He just hoped that Keisha wasn't stupid enough to have Alexis out of the closet. The officer walked Jayshawn outside to the squad car where his neighbors watched. He put him in the car and closed the door. Jayshawn looked up to see the young officer coming from inside the apartment with blood on his hands.

"I think you better call for back up," he told his partner. "We got a homicide in there."

*

Alexis sat in Dr. Rhimes office and let the tears fall as she recollected the day that she was found. The therapist sat quietly giving her the time she needed. She cried for a few more minutes and began to pull herself together.

"I'm sorry," she apologized to the therapist. "Believe it or not, despite the fact that I'm crying, I'm actually glad that I'm finally able to talk about it. It's just so hard to acknowledge sometimes. Like I still feel like this is the longest dream. People talk so much about me, but they don't know half of what I've been through. My stepfather used to tell me every day that I would never be anything. Everyone just expected me to be like my mother. My mother was intelligent and had smarts in school. She had a full scholarship to NYU and decided to chase after some man. She got pregnant with her first child when she was 17. She had to drop out of college. She had four kids after that, none of whom I really even know. She gave birth to me in a damn county jail, so what does that tell you? My father raised me because she wasn't taking care of me. She left me for a weekend with my grandmother and never came back. Who abandons their child like that? And then when I am with her, she abused me. She let that man do whatever he wanted to do to me. She took his side. She didn't say anything! She didn't stop him! What did I do that was so wrong? Why couldn't she love me?" Alexis was crying so hard it was hard to understand her. "Why?" she whispered.

Dr. Rhimes sat and allowed Alexis opportunity to cry. "I think that this is the first step into becoming a better you," he told her. "You let out a lot of tension and anger that you have been harboring for quite some time today, Alexis. You should be very proud of yourself. You got out of a situation that not a lot of people could. Not once, but twice. You have to look at what you can do versus what you can't."

Alexis listened and wiped her eyes. "You're right," she sniffed. "I just want to live a normal life. One without kidnapping, or rape, or murder," she told him.

"And you still can. You already are. You're a junior in college. And you told me you were considering pledging, right?" he asked her.

"Yea," she responded. "I was thinking about it."

Dr. Rhimes shook his head in approval. "Well, I think it would be a good step for you. You took a big step today by talking about the incident. Now the progress can truly begin. We have about five minutes left so I want to do two things. One, I'm going to give you a little assignment. I want you to write a letter to your mother. I want you to tell her everything that hurt you, bothered you, and everything that you want to say. You'll read it at one of our future sessions."

"Okay, I can do that." Alexis told him. "What's the second thing?"

"I want you to take a small step and reach out to Tamika." Dr. Rhimes saw Alexis' body language. "Okay, relax. Even if it's just a phone call, or a text message. Try to take that step. I know that you really loved her as a friend because of the pain that you are experiencing. So take that step towards a better you," he suggested.

Alexis grabbed her bag and stood to leave. "I'll think about it," she said as she walked out. *Like hell I will,* she thought, closing the door and walking to her car.

Alexis reached her car and, after getting in, opened her glove compartment to see the pills sitting there. She picked up the bottle and opened it. Changing her mind, she put the pills back in her glove box, started her car and drove away. She picked up her cell phone to three missed calls. She saw that Summer had called and decided to give her a call first. She listened to the ring back song for Summer's phone and found herself humming along.

"Everybody know it ain't trickin if you got it. Trickin if you got, trickin, if you got it. Everybody know it ain't trickin if you got it."

"Hello?" Summer answered.

"Hey, girl. What you doing?" Alexis asked.

"Girl, nothing. On my way to go out with this dude I met a few weeks ago," she told her. "What you up to?"

Alexis laughed. "Oh, lawd. I'm just now leaving this therapy session with Dr. Rhimes. About to run to the crib and pack a bag for this weekend," she answered.

"Where you going?" Summer demanded.

Alexis smiled. Her friends could not understand their friendship but Summer was Alexis' ace boon. They fought like cats and dogs, but at the end of the day, they were always there for each other. When everything happened, the minute Summer found out, she was there. All the petty stuff went out the window.

"Um, hello? I said where you going?" Summer asked again.

"I'm going to Virginia to see Henderson," she told her.

"Oh," Summer said dryly.

"Well damn, why you gotta say it like that?" Alexis asked with an attitude.

Summer sighed into the phone. "I mean, I don't like him, but do you. He too fucking cocky."

Alexis rolled her eyes and responded. "Well damn, Summer, you haven't necessarily been the nicest to him either, so what you expect?"

"Whatever. Like I said, you gonna do what you wanna do, so it's no point in me telling you otherwise," she told her.

"Anyways, so who is this nigga you going out with? While you talking about me," Alexis asked, changing the subject.

"GIRL! His name is Rodney. I met him a few weeks ago at Cheap Seats. We been texting or whatever and he supposed to be taking me to go get something to eat," her friend said, excited.

"Well damn, how you go to Cheap Seats without me?" Alexis asked, disappointed.

There was a brief pause on the phone before Summer responded. "Well, I mean, I went with Tamika. I didn't wanna call you and ask you, cause it ain't like you would've gone."

Alexis ignored her frustration and acted as if it didn't bother her. "It's cool. I mean, hell, that's your bestie…so, whatever."

Summer snapped at Alexis. "Look, don't come at me with that, Lex. You know I rock harder for you than any muthafuckin body. But I'm not gonna ignore Tamika and stop talking to her because you two ain't talking. Fact of the matter is, you wrong. Yes, I understand Tamika fucked up, but damn, we all fuck up, including yourself. You would think that everything you went through would show you how to really appreciate those that love you and care about you, but you acting like a fucking stuck up snob. Tamika is not the one that kidnapped you. Her brother was. What; you think she wanted him to do the shit? She's just as miserable as you right now and whether you wanna admit it or not, I know you miss her. So stop acting like the world owes you something and stop taking it out on us. We're your friends and we love you."

Alexis looked at the phone as if it was foreign. "Really, Summer? That's how you wanna do? I don't need this extra shit right now. I don't!" she screamed.

"Then end the shit, Lex!" Summer screamed back cutting her off. "Cause we're all tired of it and I'm not gonna be in the middle of it anymore." Alexis heard the click as Summer hung up the phone.

Alexis threw the phone in the passenger seat as she continued the drive to her house. Furious, she pulled in to the gate, showing the guard her card for access and pulled into her driveway. She opened her garage, pulled in and left her car running. She ran in to grab some clothes and to put food in Chub Chub's bowl. She remembered that she had a missed call from Henderson while she was in her session. She picked up her house phone to call. The phone rang and it went to voicemail.

"Hey, it's me, Lex. I'm grabbing some clothes from the house and then I'm hitting the highway. So, call me and let me know if everything is still good. Aight? Bye."

She hung up the phone and ran to her room, grabbing some clothes and throwing them in her duffle bag. She let her dog out for a quick walk and set his food in his bowl. She set the alarm and ran back to the garage, getting in her car. She picked up her phone and sent a text to her neighbor asking her to let the dog back in the house and to walk him while she was gone. Her phone beeped when she sat it down on the seat.

Henderson: Where u at?

Alexis: I just called you, big head. I'm on the way now. Had to stop by the house to get some clothes. I should be there in a few hrs.

Henderson: Wat # did u call me from

Alexis: My house phone. I am on the way. C u in a few.

Henderson: Aight.

Alexis put his address in her GPS, put on her Beyoncé *BDay* cd and hit the road. She decided to call Collin just to see if he was okay from earlier that day. Plus, she wanted to know who the girl was he was with. His phone rang twice and went to voicemail. She decided not to leave a voicemail and hung up. A few minutes later, her phone beeped to an incoming message from Collin.

Collin: Stop calling. I don't wanna be with you. I've moved on.

Alexis looked at the message in anger. Summer's words rang out in her head for some reason. She didn't know why, but all she heard was, "Stop acting like the world owes you something."

She turned the volume up to the max on her cd and put her foot on the gas. "I act like the world owes me something?" she said out loud. "You fucking right I do. And it's time to collect."

*

Alexis pulled up to Henderson's apartment complex and called him to let him know she was downstairs. She hadn't seen him in a year and her stomach was in knots. She couldn't believe that she was there.

"Hey, I'm here. Which apartment is it?" she asked.

"C. The door is unlocked. You need help with your stuff?" he asked her.

"Nah, I should be fine. Be up in a sec," she said.

She hung up the phone and threw it in her purse. She grabbed her overnight bag that sat in the passenger seat and alarmed her car, checking her surroundings as she walked towards the building. She looked to the top of the stairs to see Henderson standing waiting for her. She smiled and walked faster up the stairs. She got to the top and stood face to face with the man she knew in her heart she still loved.

"Long time no see," she said softly.

"Girl, shut up and come here," he demanded.

Alexis smiled at his demand as she walked into his open arms. "Same old Henderson," she said as they walked into his apartment.

He closed the door behind them and put her bag on the couch. Alexis looked around at the apartment to avoid looking at him. She felt as if she was just meeting him for the first time even though they had been talking for years. She didn't know what to expect with him.

Is he tryna work it out? she thought. What the hell am I doing here?

"I take it you like the spot?" Henderson asked her, interrupting her thoughts.

"Huh?" she asked, confused. Realizing what he said, she answered "Yea, it's nice. I mean, clearly, you can tell it's a bachelor's pad but as long as it works for you," she replied smartly.

"Whatever," Henderson said, rolling his eyes. "You can take a seat. Ain't nobody gonna bite you. Or you tryna get the grand tour?"

Alexis laughed at his sarcasm. "Nah, I think I'm good on that. After the long day that I had, plus that drive, I just wanna lay down and sleep."

Henderson walked close enough to her that their faces were almost touching. "Oh, you gonna lay down all right," he whispered and kissed her.

He backed her against the wall and kissed her longingly, wrestling her tongue with his tongue. Alexis wanted to stop him to talk about their future but all that she could let out was a moan. They kissed passionately for what seemed like an eternity before she could finally break free to catch her breath.

"Ok, wait. Um, as much as I am enjoying this, what…what are we doing? I mean, like, are we back together or is this just a weekend thing? What?" Alexis asked softly.

Henderson stepped back, putting some space in between them. "I mean, I ain't tryna jump right back into a relationship like that. It's been over a year since me and you was together and we didn't have the typical relationship. You blamed me for the shit that went down with them muthafuckas. That shit was fucked up, Lex. I'm not saying I don't wanna be with you, but it's just not some overnight stuff," he said.

Alexis was surprised at his response. "I understand. And I know that was really messed up of me to put that all on you. Honestly, I don't blame you. I was just so mad at everything, Henderson. I needed you and you weren't there! I mean, it wasn't your fault but I just didn't know what else to do, so I blamed you. I know it's stupid and I'm sorry," Alexis apologized as she felt the tears stinging her eyes.

Henderson fidgeted as he watched her as she cried. "I wanted to be there, Lex. I didn't know what the hell was going on. If I had known you were right next door the whole time with them muthafuckas, I would have been run up in his spot. And you know his ass would be fucking dead instead of being in prison. I can't change what happened. And you know this. I'm not gonna baby you. I'm not that type of nigga. But, I can try to be more understanding. But that don't mean I'm gonna be all sentimental and shit," he told her.

Alexis sniffled, "I don't expect you to. I just don't wanna be going through this again with you if we just gonna go back to the same old BS."

"I know. I mean what do you want, Lex? Cause it ain't shit I can do about what happened. Like you keep expecting me to just go back in time or something," Henderson said, frustrated.

"I don't!" Alexis snapped. "But damn, you just fucking let me the fuck go after everything that happened. After all that bullshit, you cheated! It was like everything was for nothing!" Alexis yelled at him. "I got my ass raped and damn near killed because of your fucking baby mama!"

Henderson looked at her like she was delusional. "Last time I checked, my baby mama as crazy as she may fucking be, was not the only one there. That nigga Jayshawn was involved, too. He wanted your ass and let it be known in the goddamn courthouse in front of everybody how you switched your ass around him all the time and had all these niggas in and out your apartment. I mean, shit, Lex. You was fucking a nigga right before me and from what it sounds like, when we was together, so what the fuck you expect me to do?"

Alexis slapped Henderson hard. "Oh, so it's my fault? Did you really just say that? How the fuck is it my fault? I am so SICK of hearing how everything is my fault. It was my fault that your twisted ass baby mama and my next door neighbor decided to torture me for DAYS and that bitch damn near killed me. Oh, but I guess it's my fault. It's my fault that I was doing the exact same thing that niggas do to females BEFORE I got with you. But I guess it's my fault that you cheated on me with some random hoe. You cheated. Not me. I didn't start fucking around with Justin until AFTER we broke up. And need I remind you, we broke up because some bitch texted my phone sending you a message."

"Are we really doing this shit now?" Henderson asked, interrupting her.

"Oh no. No! You basically just told me that it was my fault for everything that happened," Alexis continued. "So yes, we are doing this. Despite what you may think, I never messed with anybody else while we were together. I loved you and even now still do. But it's my fault. Everything is always my fault. My being molested as a child, my mother letting her husband fuck me like I was okay with it. Getting me pregnant and then beating my ass because he fucking put a baby in me and got everybody thinking I'm a slut at thirteen. It's my fault that my life is so fucked up!" she cried out, breaking down.

Henderson sat looking confused at everything he'd heard. *What the fuck?* he thought to himself. *Did she just say she had a baby?* He wanted to ask her what the hell she was talking about but looking at her, she was a mess. He did the only thing he could think to do. He put his arms around her as she cried. She wanted him to be there, and he was going to try his best to do that. But they had some things to talk about it.

*

CHAPTER FIVE

Jayshawn sat in his cell waiting for the guards to come and get him. It was visitation day and after being in the hole for three weeks, he didn't give a fuck who came to see him. He knew the only one that would come to visit him though would be Ariane. She had been the only one really keeping him tight in the prison. He always had money on his books, and she would write letters that would always have some type of nasty pictures in them. The last time she was there, she paid Ricks, the one guard he was cool with, off so he would let them use one of the rooms. He only had ten minutes but he fucked all his anger and aggression out on her. He was pissed off when he got out the hole and found out Ricks was on vacation because Jayshawn needed to fuck.

The buzzing of the doors opening came down the hall, letting Jayshawn know that the guards were on the way to his cell to get him. "On your feet!" he heard the guard tell the inmates in his block. Jayshawn stood to his feet and walked to the door of his cell to wait for the guards to open the cell. The doors opened and Jayshawn walked down the hallway to be searched before he was escorted to the visitation room.

"Do you have any weapons or illegal contraband on you?" the guard asked as he began his search.

"No," Jayshawn answered dryly.

The guard finished his search and Jayshawn was free to go. He walked past a group of guards that were leaning against the wall complaining about budget cuts.

"If the state keeps cutting the budget like this, I don't see how we gonna be able to keep operating in here," the one guard said.

"Hell, fuck operating in here, if they keep doing these budget cuts, how in the fuck am I gonna be able to pay bills? I just fucking got married and we got twins on the way. I'm putting my life on the line dealing with these fucks in here. So fuck what the state gonna do to them," he told his co-worker.

Jayshawn walked past them slowly, listening to their conversation. "Move it along, inmate!" the guard told him. Jayshawn smirked and continued to walk to the visitation hall.

Jayshawn walked into the visitation hall to see Ariane sitting at one of the tables. He took in her appearance. She was dressed in a white dress and her titties were sitting up and large. Jayshawn frowned at the thought of not being able to fuck. He walked closer and noticed her face. He couldn't place it, but something was different. Ariane looked around until she saw him. She smiled as she stood.

What the fuck? he thought to himself as she stood up and he immediately noticed her stomach. He looked at her face full of excitement as he approached her. She grabbed him and hugged him. He didn't respond and sat down at the table.

"Baby!" she said happily. "I'm so glad that I get to see you. I came a few weeks ago, but they said that you were in the hole and couldn't have any visitors that week. Oh my God, I'm glad you're out. Are you okay? It's so much I wanna tell you!"

"Oh yea?" he asked. "Tell me what? Like who the fuck got you pregnant? And why the fuck you up in here throwing it in my face?"

Ariane sat back, confused at what he just said. "What?" she asked. "What you mean who got me pregnant? I'm not throwing it in your face, baby, I swear. I wanted to tell you before but I didn't know how. That's why I stopped coming for a while and I was only writing you. I know it's sudden but, in about 3 months, we're gonna have a baby," she said as she smiled rubbing her belly.

Jayshawn thought back to when he and Ariane snuck into one of the storage rooms and he busted all in her. *Damn*, he thought.

"So, what? You want me to be excited about this?" he asked her.

Ariane was no longer happy and was on the verge of tears. "Well, yea. I mean, I thought that you said you loved me and that you wanted me to have your baby," she said.

"Yea, but not while I'm in prison, dumb ass. How the fuck am I gonna be a daddy and I'm in fucking prison for ten years, Ariane?" he asked her, surprised at how naïve she was.

Ariane flinched at Jayshawn's harshness. "I'm sorry," she told him. "But, baby, it's not like I did this myself. I mean, how was I supposed to know that I was gonna get pregnant?" she asked defensively.

"Why the fuck weren't you on birth control?" he asked. "How the fuck you expect me to take care of my kid and I'm in here? How the fuck do I know that's even my baby? For all I know, you can be playing me."

Ariane sat back and got angry. "Wait a minute, I know you not tryna say that I'm out here fucking around," she spat. "I mean, let's be real, Jay. I have been down for you since day one. Even when you fucked that other bitch and got put the fuck in here, I STILL went hard for you. I put money on your books and paid your attorney with my money that I had for college. I have done everything you have asked," she said trying hard not to cry.

Jayshawn grabbed her arm tightly, to the point where she was in pain. She tried to cry out but he hushed her. "Don't even do it. Don't EVER fucking come at me like that again," he said in a harsh whisper. "And stop them fucking tears." He eased his grip on her arm and put the guilt trip on her. "You sitting here talking about how you ride for me when it's because of your ass that I'm in here. YOU the one that called the cops and filed assault charges on me. Because of you, the cops came to my house and fuckin' arrested my ass. Because of you, Keisha is dead. So, am I supposed to be thanking you right now? Huh?" he asked.

Ariane sat quiet and felt horrible. "Well, what do you want me to do?" she asked in a whisper.

"I want you to stop playing the damn pity party. You talking about you wanna ride for me and all that, then you need to get with the program. Stop all this damn crying all the time. That shit is fucking annoying," he said.

Ariane sniffed and said, "Okay."

"Okay, what?" Jayshawn asked with a grin.

Ariane smiled slowly. "Okay, daddy."

Jayshawn smiled. He loved the fact that Ariane was so easily controlled. "That's what I like to hear. Don't worry. You know I love you. But you gotta own up to your part in this. I'm gonna fix this but, eventually, you gonna have to get your hands a little dirty, too," he told her.

If you only knew how dirty I'm getting for you, she thought to herself.

Jayshawn looked up to see the two guards he overheard earlier walking by. He thought about his guard on the inside and wondered if the budget cuts would affect him, too. He hoped that it did because it would make it easy for him to work on getting out of there.

"I need you to do something for me. It'll be a big way for us to be together soon," he told Ariane.

She immediately sat up and listened. "Anything, baby. What do you need?" she asked.

"Do you remember Ricks, the guard you paid for us to go to that storage room the last time?" he asked her.

"Of course," she answered.

"Good. He's got an attorney that may be able to find a way for me to get my sentence reduced or knocked off due to technicality. But he needs $5,000 to make it happen," he told her.

"Okay. Well, I mean I only have about $2,000 in my savings that I have for the baby," She told him, confused. "Besides, what's up with your attorney? I just gave him some money last week."

Jayshawn frowned. "Didn't I just tell you about that? See, that's what I'm talking about. I'm telling you I got an opportunity for us to be together so that I can be there for you and this baby and this is what you do? I think you want to be alone. Maybe you should try that," he said, letting her hand go.

Ariane reached for him. "No! No, baby, I'm in. Just tell me what you need," she pleaded.

"I need $5,000. Can you do it?" he asked.

"Yes. I'm gonna come up with the money, but it may take a few months," she told him.

Jayshawn thought about Meech, his connect in Charlotte, and decided to hit him up when he got the chance. "Nah. All I need you to do is take that $2,000 to a friend of mine named Meech in Charlotte. I will let him know you are coming. He is gonna give you a box to take with you. Don't open it. Just take it to Mo, my nigga in the boro. He'll take it and give you $10,000 by the end of the week. I'm gonna call you at the end of the week and make sure everything is cool. Then, when you come for another visit, you'll give the money to Ricks and everything will be taken care of. Okay?" he instructed her.

"Okay," she answered eagerly. "I can do that."

"Good," he replied. "So, is it a boy or girl?" he asked, curious.

Ariane smiled at his curiosity. "I don't know yet. I figured we could be surprised."

"Well, I want a boy," he told her. "I already got a son with my baby mama so that better be a boy in there. Gotta carry on my legacy."

Ariane gave a nervous laugh. *My child will not be in prison,* she thought to herself. "Well, we'll find out soon enough," she said.

"Yea," he said, no longer interested. "Just don't get stupid like her and you'll be aight."

"I won't," she promised.

"Two minutes!" the guard yelled out, letting the inmates and visitors know that they had two minutes before the time was up so everyone could say their goodbyes and finish their visits.

Jayshawn stood up to get ready to leave. "Remember what I said," he told her. "Don't fuck this up." He opened his arms and let Ariane hug him.

"Don't worry baby. I'll take care of everything," she told him.

He watched her walk off and noticed most of the male guards looking at her and her now larger ass. The pregnancy had done her body good because she was thick everywhere and filling out nicely. He smirked at their stares. *She could really work to my advantage,* he thought and walked back to his cell with a little pep in his step.

*

It had been the longest week of Jayshawn's life as he waited for Ricks to come back from vacation. He did everything in his cell except eat to make sure he did not find a way to get in trouble. He stayed out of all the guard's way and was on his best behavior. He finally spotted Ricks in the cafeteria when he was leaving to throw his tray in the trash. He motioned for him to let him know that he needed to talk to him.

"Cheston!" Ricks yelled at him. "You have not been dismissed. Did anyone tell you to get up?"

Jayshawn stood and played his role. "Man, I'm done. Quit fucking sweating me."

Ricks walked over to him and grabbed him by his collar. "That's it. Let's go!" he walked Jayshawn to the same storage room that he fucked Ariane in. "Man, what's up?" he whispered.

"I heard y'all had some budget cuts," Jayshawn told him.

Ricks took a few steps back. "Really? You did all this to ask me about some fucking budget cuts?" he asked.

Jayshawn let out a laugh. "I'm saying. I got something that I think may work in your favor."

Ricks was now interested. "Alright. Go ahead, I'm listening," he said.

"I think I may have a way to supplement some of your lost income. Word is that the state is cutting the budget, and may be getting rid of some of y'all. I know that this is going to affect your pay. And I know you got a fam to take care of, and I'm trying to get up out of here," Jayshawn told him.

"So what? You trying to pay me to sneak you out of here?" Ricks asked, confused.

"Nah, nothing like that. But I do happen to know that I can get you $5000 in a matter of three days. All I ask is that you look the other way," Jayshawn answered confidently.

"I don't know about that," Ricks said, uneasy.

"What? Are you scared? I'm saying, bruh think about this. My girl can bring you the $5,000 and all you gotta do is look the other way." He answered.

"Yea, but how? I can't just walk you the hell up out of here," Ricks whispered.

Jayshawn laughed. "Bruh, I know that. But I know that y'all ship the guards' uniforms out of here for cleaning every Wednesday, so I'll conveniently be on laundry duty that day. But you need to make sure that that happens. And no one will know. Just make sure that you put yourself on watch in the laundry area and look out for your boy. Once I'm on the outside, I could make sure that you're set," he told him.

Rick thought about Jayshawn's proposition. "$5000, huh?" he said. "Damn, I definitely could use that right now. Hell, I don't plan on being here much longer anyway."

"All the more better," Jayshawn said. "So you in?" he asked.

Ricks thought about it for a minute. With the budget cuts, he knew that he was at risk to be laid off. "Alright, cool. I'm in."

Jayshawn grinned, shaking his head in agreement. "Good. I'm going to call my girl today and let her know that on next visitation day she needs to come a few minutes early. She's going to come and see you and give you $5,000. So you need to make sure that you search her bag. Act like you see something and pull her in for a private search," he instructed.

The good thing about the prison and the budget cuts is that it was 98% males that worked at the facility. They only had two female guards and they worked the gate. So the chances of Ariane getting searched by a man were great. Jayshawn looked at Ricks seriously. "Make sure that you hold up your end of the bargain, and you'll be good. I got people that can look out for you. But if you fuck me, you will regret it."

Ricks nodded his head in agreement. "Just remember, I'm doing you a favor. Inmate," he emphasized. He opened the door and looked out to make sure that the coast was clear. He walked out the door and went on with his shift thinking about the money that was about to be in his pocket in a few days. He definitely needed it since he was probably going to be one of the guards that was cut because of the budget. He figured it would hold him over for a while. A few minutes later, Jayshawn walked out of the storage room and walk back towards his cell, smiling at the plan that was underway.

*

Four days had passed and Jayshawn sat in the recreation room awaiting visitation. He could practically smell the freedom he was about to have. No one else would be telling him when to get up, or shower, or eat. He would be able to do any and everything he wanted to do. And one of those things on his to do list would be to kill Alexis; but not until he had some more fun with her. He was playing cards with one of his friends from a different block, but he wasn't really paying attention. He kept looking at the clock. Right about now, Ariane was arriving and going through security. He hoped that she did exactly what he told her to do and hoped that Ricks was following the plan. He looked at the guard standing at the front of the door and smile. *Soon,* he thought. *Real soon.*

*

Ariane walked into the prison for visitation day with the money in her bra. *Thank God I'm pregnant and my titties are bigger,* she thought to herself. She made sure she put the new pack of lady razors in her purse to give Ricks the idea she had a weapon as Jayshawn told her to do.

Ricks looked at Ariane as she walked through the metal detector. She was wearing a royal blue maxi halter dress that accentuated her body. *Damn this nigga is lucky as hell*, he thought to himself. He couldn't keep his eyes off of her. He was trying not to stare, but just looking at her was making his dick hard. *Might as well have a little bit of fun*, he thought as he decided to try to fuck.

"I'm sorry, ma'am, but I'm going to have to search you. Because of the items in your bag, it requires a search. Would you please follow me into the room?" he instructed.

Ricks walked down the hallway as if he was walking to the interrogation room. He had already unlocked the door to the storage unit next door where he and Jayshawn met previously. He didn't want it obvious that he was taking money. He walked into the room and quickly pulled Ariane in it.

"I understand you're supposed to have something for me?" he asked her. Ariane nodded her head up and down in agreement. She pulled out a roll of hundreds totaling $5,000 out of her bra. No longer being able to avoid it, he looked to where her hands were reaching. It was almost as if she was drawing attention to them on purpose. She handed him the roll and he put it in his pocket.

"I believe that is all?" she asked him.

Smiling a very sneaky smile he said, "No. We're not finished yet." He backed her against the door, placing his hands on her breasts.

Ariane was confused and it showed on her face. "What are you talking about? Jay said all I had to do was come here and give you the money. What else is there?" she asked in a shaky voice.

Ricks placed his hand over her mouth to silence her. "You know what you're supposed to do. Your boy said that I could get some. After all, it is his freedom at stake. Or do you want him to stay here locked up?" he asked.

Ariane stood, eyes welling with tears. "But," she said, "he didn't tell me to do that. He said bring the money to you and that you would help him out."

Ricks stood looking agitated. "Look, do you want him to get out or not? I guess not. Move," he told her, pushing her to the side.

"No! No, I don't want him in here. I'll do it," she replied reluctantly.

Ricks smiled, unbuckling his pants. He pulled her titties out from her dress and began sucking on them as she raised the bottom of her dress up.

"Just please don't hurt my baby," she told him as she rubbed her stomach.

Ricks grabbed her hands and put them at her side. "Don't worry. This ain't gonna hurt at all. This gonna have you wanting more." He pulled his dick out and placed it inside of her.

Ariane tried to relax but all she wanted to do was cry because she was so mad. *How could he do this to me? How could he do this to our baby,* she thought to herself as Ricks continued to fuck her. Ricks grinded her with heavy force and speed and, judging by his grunts, he was enjoying it.

"Damn, you got some good pussy," he told her. "I see why this nigga keep you around. Too bad you wasting this bomb ass pussy on a nigga like him."

Ariane tried to contain her anger as she felt him pushing his way into her. She tried to relax and act as if she was enjoying it. She imagined he was Jayshawn and let out a few moans. She would do anything to please Jayshawn and to make up what she had done. She leaned back against the table and let Ricks fuck her in a position that would make him come faster.

"Damn, this is some good ass pussy," he said again as he kept pumping. He continued to push in and out of her, trying to contain himself from coming. *I can't believe she actually fell for it. I'm gonna have fun with this. Make her bust for a real nigga*, he thought. He squeezed her titties and, unable to hold back anymore, got ready to come. *Might as well, shit she already pregnant*, he thought to himself. Ariane felt him release inside of her. He'd fucked her so hard he was sweating.

"Damn!" was all he could say. He pulled his pants back up and wiped his forehead. He looked around and found a roll of tissue and gave it to Ariane to clean herself up.

"Are we good?" she asked as she snatched it from him.

"Oh yeah, we good, baby. Just make sure you keep your mouth shut," he told her. "Don't say shit to that nigga about what just happened or I'll make sure he die in this muthafucka."

"Wait a minute," she said, realizing what was just said. "I thought you said that Jayshawn agreed to this?"

"Yeah, well, I lied," He laughed. He got close enough to her that their noses were touching. "But like I just told you, keep your fucking mouth shut and this nigga will be fine. But if you say anything to him, then I'm gonna make sure this nigga never get out of this bitch. And your ass might end up having your baby in prison for bringing in illegal contraband do; you understand?" he asked her.

"Oh, I understand," she answered. If she could kill him right, there she would have. But she knew how she could get him. "Well now that I know what I'm getting, you know I'm gonna have to get that again," she said flirtatiously.

"Shit, we can go again now!" Ricks said eagerly.

Ariane laughed at his eagerness. "Not now, otherwise he'll get suspicious." She played with him. "But I will just call you so we can get up," she suggested.

"Cool," he agreed. He wrote his number down and slid it inside of her bra as he got one last feel on her full breasts. "Okay, now fix yourself up. We need to get back out there," he told her.

Ariane fixed her dress back to the way it was since he'd messed it up pulling on it. Ricks walked out, walking several paces ahead of her back to the visitation area. He walked to his coworkers and superiors to let them know that she had passed the body inspection and everything was okay. Ariane proceeded to sit down at the table to wait for Jayshawn. Almost immediately, he walked in, passing Ricks and Ariane smiled.

Ricks winked and gave her a quick grin. She smiled back. *Trust muthafucka*, she thought to herself, *you gonna get yours.* Ariane was so pissed but she had to smile in front of Jayshawn. But soon, she knew she would get her chance to get him back. She couldn't wait to torture him and let Jayshawn watch.

Jayshawn sat down at the table and immediately begin asking her questions. "Did you get it done?" he asked her.

"Of course," she said with a smile. "Trust me, he'll be well taken care of," she said to him with a certain hint of malice.

"Good. Then in a couple of days, I'll be out of here. You know what you need to do next, right?" he asked, making sure that she knew the plan.

"Yes, baby. I'm going to pick you up from at the McDonald's off exit 135 with a change of clothes. My brother is going to let you stay with him for a couple of days until we can get you an apartment. He's going to put the apartment in his name so that way you're not drawing attention to yourself. Oh, and when I went to see Meech, he said to come see him when you get out and he'll throw some paper at you to hold you down for a while," she remembered.

"Cool," he told her. "Everything will be fine soon. I'm going to tie up some loose ends and then we're getting the hell out of North Carolina," he told her. "Maybe move to Atlanta or to Miami."

"Atlanta would be great!" She said. "They have great hair schools there and I know I could make a lot of money in Atlanta."

"That's what I'm banking on," he said to her. "Alright, so just make sure that you stick to everything that you're supposed to do and everything will be fine," he told her.

"Don't worry, baby. I got you. And I got a lot of surprises for you, too, when you get out." She knew that he would be happy that she was getting rid of the reason that he was in there in the first place. She knew it was her fault for calling the cops for the assault charge, but if Alexis had never come around, none of this would be happening now. She had already gotten rid of Collin, so she would get rid of Alexis for him. He would definitely love her then. She smiled at the thought of them being together again.

"Cheston, time's up!" Ricks yelled.

Ariane looked pissed. "But we just started," she protested.

"And now you're ending," Ricks told her. "Cheston, back to your cell."

Jayshawn looked at Ariane and told her to relax. "It's all part of the plan. I'm getting in trouble so that I can go to the laundry duty for the next few days. Don't worry," he whispered. "Just play it cool." He gave her a kiss on her cheek and walked off.

Ariane sat there pissed off. Even though he told her that it was a part of the plan, she really was upset. She had been through way too much that day. Getting up out of her chair and walking out of the visitation room to her car, she thought, *I hope I don't ever have to come back to this muthafucka.* She started her car and drove away to complete her plans. She had 48 hours to get rid of Alexis.

Jayshawn walked down the hallway with Ricks. "She took care of you?" he asked just to make sure.

"Oh yeah. She took real good care of me," Rick responded. Ricks walked towards the guard's booth with Jayshawn.

"What did this asshole do?" one of the guards asked.

"Failure to comply with guards' orders. Therefore, we had to end his visitation. I'm putting him on laundry duty for the next week since he wants to be belligerent. Get your ass in there, inmate! I want those fucking loads done, ASAP!" he ordered Jayshawn.

Jayshawn snatched away from Ricks and walked into the laundry room to begin his new duties. Ricks stood and continued to talk to the guards at the booth.

"Don't you have a kid with a birthday party this week?" he asked the guard.

"Yeah. I'm supposed to be taking the kids to Chuck E. Cheese's on Wednesday, but the fucking warden has me working here with these ingrates," he answered.

Ricks jumped at the opportunity. "Hey why don't you go ahead and take off and I'll cover for you? Besides, I need the overtime," he asked.

"Really?" the guard asked him.

"Yeah," he replied. "I got you covered."

"Man, I appreciate it. I didn't know what my wife was going to say if I couldn't make it. This is great," the guard said thanking him.

"No problem," Ricks said. "No problem at all. We all gotta stick together."

He stuck his hands in his pockets, feeling the financial gain he had just received and walked off to head back to his post with a smile on his face.

*

First Lady K

CHAPTER SIX

Dear Mom,

I'm writing you because my therapist thinks it's a good idea for me to release some of this anger that I have. He thinks that it's a good way for me to change some of my behavior. I honestly don't even know where to begin. But I hate you. I hate you for everything that you did to me, and everything that you let be done to me. I try so hard to live my life and do everything right that you didn't do, and to be everything that you weren't. Sometimes, I hope that I never have children because I'm scared that if I do, I may turn out like you.

I don't understand what I did to you. I was just a little girl. What did I do that was so wrong that would allow you to let somebody hurt me like that? How could you hate me so much? I don't have any happy memories of us. It's bad that the only memories I have are you yelling at me, or hitting me, or letting your husband do whatever he wanted to do with me. I begged you so many times to let me go live with my daddy and you told me that he didn't want me. You told me that he wasn't shit. But anytime but I saw him all he would do was let me know how much I was loved by him, and that his door was open for me at any time to live with him. How can you be so cruel? I always ask myself even to this day how a woman can keep her children from their father. And then make me call somebody that was abusive and a fucking rapist my father? He was NOT my father. He did not treat me like a daughter; he treated me like a whore. And you let it happen.

I don't know if you're in heaven or hell, but I hope that you know what you did to me. Because of you, I can't trust anybody. Because of you, I have nightmares to this day. I've been through more than you will ever imagine. Do you know I tried to kill myself because of the entire trauma? I don't know if you're having a way of seeing it because you're not here, but I have done a lot with my life. It may not be all that I'm supposed to be doing; the one thing that you did teach me is that I can use my looks to my advantage.

I'm in school getting a degree; something you couldn't do. I don't have three or four babies by three or four different men. I have no children by choice. I'm taking care of me. I'm living a successful life doing what I want to do. I may not do everything the way it should be done but it's being done. Writing this, it does help me to get out my frustration because as a child you shut me up all the time. You only gave me attention when we were out in public and you were making sure that I never told your secret. Were you that desperate for a husband? Were you that desperate for a man? That you would just let him do whatever he wanted to do with your children. And for the longest, I thought it was something that I did wrong.

It wasn't until I got older and my father was the one that had to tell me that no, it's not my fault. That that man was sick. And I hope that he is somewhere rotting in hell where he deserves to be. I'm glad that I killed your husband. He deserved to die. And the fact that you put me out and sent me to live with my father because I put the man that was abusing your daughter in the ground and I told you and the judge told you it was in self-defense? I could have died. It shouldn't have ever gotten to that point! If I had known that that was a way for me to live with my father I would have done it a long time ago! I hate you! You did this to me. But I'm not going to allow you to have any more control over my life anymore.

Although you have not physically been on this earth for quite some time you still had a hold on me and I just didn't realize it until I started writing this letter. So thank you. Thank you for putting me through all of that because it's making me a stronger person now. I only hope that when I do get married eventually, that the man can deal with everything that I've been through. I only hope that if I do become a mother one day, although I am very apprehensive about it, then my child will understand that I love them. Because I'm going to let it be known every single day. I'm not going to choke my child or raise my hands to my child when I'm frustrated. I'm not going to take my frustrations out on my kid because I don't have anyone else or can't handle my problems like an adult. I'm not going to pass my child off to my husband as some type of sexual favor. Anybody that does that is sick. And they deserve to be locked up or dead. But you know what? I'm good. Because I'm going to be better.

I'm going to be better for me. I'm going to prove you and everybody else who thought I was going to end up like you wrong. It's hard because there are many days where I think about you and I will start crying. I cry because I hear of other girls' relationships with their mothers. How close they are, and how we were never that. I think one of the main reasons I was so hurt when you passed away was because I didn't get a chance to tell you about all the resentment that I had for you. I didn't get a chance to let you know exactly how you hurt me. But now that I have the opportunity, I can let it go. I can let go of all the pain. Because I know that it was not my fault like you led me to believe. I know that I did not cause this. I know that you married the wrong person. I know that you were the one that let this happen. And unfortunately, I was not smart enough at the time to know that it was not my fault and believed you.

Sadly, I can't even fault you because I knew what kind of childhood you had. You lived with verbal abuse and learned to be like the one woman you hated. But now that I'm older and now that I know better, all I can do is hope that if you're able to hear this, and that you will know the damage that you've done. But I'm not going to let it control me any longer. I gotta break the cycle. I'm going to live my life to the fullest, with no regrets!

Goodbye, mother.

*

Alexis finished her letter and put the pen down. She had tears in her eyes as she sat in her condo. She had been with Summer most of the day and they were back at it as if nothing ever happened. They had fallen out before and she was sure they would again. But that was just how they were. Alexis looked at her phone and saw that she had no new notifications. She looked next to her phone and saw a piece of paper with a phone number on it from someone she'd met a few days prior at the gym.

His name was Malik Davis and although he was a little older, Alexis definitely wanted to keep him on speed dial. He was 38 and was an attorney for one of the largest law firms in Raleigh. He'd told her he was single but she saw the wedding band tan line on his finger and knew that it was a lie. But it didn't matter to her. She wasn't trying to fall in love. She was going to get him to be her new sugar daddy. *Hell, it's not my fault his wife ain't handling business,* she thought to herself. Picking up her phone, she texted him to see if he was free.

Alexis: Hey cutie. I got home and thought about how great it was meeting you last night.

Before she could put the phone down, he had already responded. She laughed at his eagerness. "Like candy from a baby." she said out loud as she read his message.

Malik: Well, hello there, beautiful. How are you today?

Alexis: I'm good. Just got in from hanging out with one of my friends on campus. How are you today?

Malik: Now that I'm talking to you I'm doing very well. When will I get the opportunity to see you again?

Alexis: That sounds great. And as far as to when you'll see me again, what is your schedule like? I'm sure the life of an attorney is very busy.

Malik: Never too busy to spend time with a beautiful lady. ☺

He really thinks he has game, she thought. Isn't that cute.

Alexis: Very smooth, Malik. Well when would you like to get up? And where would you be taking me?

Malik: Anywhere you want to go, princess. Whatever will keep that beautiful smile on your face.

Malik: How about we go to Mimi's Cafe? It's a little small but their food is wonderful and the ambiance is great.

Alexis: I'd like that. When?

Malik: How about now?

Alexis: Well aren't you in a hurry? Now would not be a good time, however, I am free this evening…

Malik: That would be wonderful, Ms. Thomas. I look forward to seeing you. Would you like me to pick you up? Or would you prefer that we meet at the restaurant?

Alexis: For now we can meet at the restaurant. But who knows, perhaps in the future you may be able to pick me up in your chariot. ☺

Malik: Well I will definitely look forward to the future. And I definitely look forward to getting to know you a lot better, Ms. Thomas. Until tonight...

Alexis: Until tonight, sir.

She put her phone down, smiling as she got up to find something that would accentuate every single curve she worked hard in the gym four days a week to keep. She decided on a black peplum leather skirt and red blouse with lace sleeves. She laid the clothes at the end of her bed and made sure that she put aside a cute bra and panty set. She didn't plan on sleeping with him but she definitely wanted him to see what was underneath. She heard her phone go off on the desk. Walking across the room, she picked it up to see a text message from Summer.

Summer: Hey have you started the application yet?

Alexis had forgotten about the application for Delta. She and Summer decided that they were going to pledge their senior year.

Alexis: Thanx for reminding me, I'm about to start it now. Girl I fell asleep! Lol.

Summer: Well wake your ass up and fill out that application!

Alexis: Lol. I'm on it.

Alexis pulled the application out of her backpack and sat down on the bed looking it over. She began to fill out the application and reading over the requirements that were necessary to join. She knew her father would be ecstatic since he was in their brother fraternity, so she didn't want to tell him until she was selected. She looked at the price and thought about getting her new soon-to-be sugar daddy to sponsor her. She set her clock so that she could get up later to prepare for her date and finished her application.

*

Alexis woke up to her alarm clock going off. She got up going into the bathroom to turn her shower on and check her phone. She saw she had some messages from a few of the guys that she used to fuck with that were trying to get up with her. Deleting the messages, she decided to reach out and call Collin. She hadn't heard from him and it was almost as if he had disappeared. She just knew he would have responded to her texts or phone calls by now. She called his phone and it went straight to voicemail again. She decided not to leave a message.

"Oh well, his loss," she said as she took her clothes off to get in the shower. No sooner had she stepped in than she heard glass breaking. She jumped out of the shower, grabbing her towel and wrapping it around her body. She kept a gun in her bathroom drawer. Grabbing it, she went into the living room where the noise came from. It was there where she found a rock with a piece of paper attached to it. She picked up the rock, careful not to step on any glass and pulled the paper that was attached to it off.

You're dead bitch, the note read.

What the fuck? Alexis thought. Are you fucking kidding me?

Alexis checked the rest of the house to make sure that no one had gotten in. She went to her room and grabbed her cell phone, calling the police.

"911, what's your emergency?" the operator answered.

Alexis, trying to remain calm, let her know that someone had thrown a rock through her living room window. She explained that no one else was in the home with her and the dispatcher told her to stay on the phone until police arrived. She heard the sirens in the distance within seconds. The one thing about Alexis' neighborhood that she checked before she moved in was the response time for police and fire.

How in the hell did they get past the gate? she questioned. Alexis went into her room to put some clothes on. She always kept a pair of clothes in the chair by her dresser in case she needed to make a quick escape. She contemplated calling her father but decided against since she knew he would make her leave. The police came to the door and Alexis answered their questions as they checked the inside and outside of her home.

"Miss Thomas, do you know of anyone that may want to do this to you?" one of the officers asked.

"No," she told him. "I just moved here last year and no one knows where I live except a few people." She heard her phone ringing and looked down to see Malik calling her. She had completely forgotten she was supposed to be meeting him for dinner.

"Hey, Malik," she answered. "I'm so sorry. I know I was supposed to meet you for dinner tonight. Unfortunately, I had an incident at my condo and the police are here getting everything fixed," she said in a shaky voice.

"What's the matter?" Malik asked, concerned.

"Oh, it's nothing big. One of my windows was broken and it's standard procedure to call the police when it is in this development," she lied.

"Are you okay?" he asked her. "You weren't hurt, were you?" The concern was evident in his tone.

"No I'm fine. I was in the shower getting ready when it happened. The noise scared me, of course, but other than that, I'm okay," she reassured him.

"Well, are they coming to fix your window tonight? What's your address? I can come and get you and get you in a hotel or something so that you're comfortable while they do the repairs," he offered.

Alexis was surprised at his hospitality. "No, really, it's okay," she said. "It's just a small window. They should be able to fix it soon."

"Nonsense," he said. "What kind of man would I be knowing that I have the ability to help a damsel in distress?"

The police were waiting on her to hang up the phone so that they could finish the questions. Alexis hesitated and agreed that Malik could help to him hurry off the phone. After giving him her address, they hung up the phone and Alexis continued to answer the officers' questions.

"Ms. Thomas, does anyone know the code to get into your gate?" he asked.

"No," she answered. "You have to have a badge or your name has to be on the visitation list. They don't just let anyone in here."

"Well, apparently, someone was let in today," the officer informed her. "You may want to speak to your property management to let them know what's going on as well. We'll talk to the security guards when we leave to see what they know and what they may have seen."

Their conversation was interrupted by a knock at her door. She went to the door to open it, assuming that it was Malik. Instead, in her door stood a tall white man in a suit.

"Can I help you?" she asked.

"Yes, I'm looking for an Alexis Thomas," he told her.

"I'm Alexis. Who are you?" she frowned.

The man showed his badge. "My name is Detective Williams. I need to speak to you." The detective looked around to see the officers in her living room. "Ms. Thomas, it is urgent that I speak with you," the detective stated.

"Why? Do you know something about the window?" she asked, confused.

"I'm not here about your window," the detective told her. "I'm here regarding a Collin Strong. I need to ask you some questions."

What the hell? she thought to herself. "Yes, please come in," she responded.

The detective asked the officers to step out.

"Absolutely," they told him. "Ms. Thomas, we will be outside speaking with your security. Remember to check with your property manager in the morning. If you can think of anything else, please give us a call," the officer said.

The officers walked out and shut the door behind them while Alexis sat down on the couch. "What's going on? Why are you asking me about Collin?" she asked.

The detective sat down in the chair across from her and begin telling her his reason for being there. "Ms. Thomas, I'm coming to you because upon finding Mr. Strong's phone tonight, a call came in. That incoming call was you. When was the last time you spoke with Mr. Strong?" he inquired.

Alexis looked nervous. "It's been a while," she answered. "He and I have not spoken in over a month."

"I see. And what exactly was your relation to Mr. Strong?" he asked her.

"He and I dated," she replied. "We were together for about a year but we broke up a few months ago."

"So you have not spoken to him since? Have you seen him since then?" he asked her.

"I saw him about a month after we broke up, on campus. I tried to call him but he never called me back. Why; what's going on?" Alexis asked, now scared.

The detective wrote down the information she gave him and closed his notepad. He sighed, knowing the news he had to deliver. "Ms. Thomas, I hate to be the one to tell you this, but we found Mr. Strong's body last night. Coroner says he died of a gunshot wound to the back of the head. From what we know already, he's been gone for a while."

Alexis had to register what was just told to her. "Wait, what did you say? No… That can't be. He can't be dead," she said, shaky.

"I'm sorry," he told her. "I know this is hard to deal with. The coroner said based off decomposition, that he has been dead for at least a month. We are working to find out what happened. Do you know if he had any enemies? Was there anyone that he had disagreements with?"

Alexis heard the detective asking her the question but she still couldn't process that Colin was gone. "He can't be. He can't be dead. How could this happen?" she rambled off. "No! No!" She screamed again. Alexis broke down in tears. Her phone began to ring but she didn't bother to answer. The detective looked at the phone and saw Summer's name on the caller ID.

"Ms. Thomas would you like me to get that?" He asked.

Alexis could do nothing but shake her head and cry and repeatedly whisper, "no." She felt as if everything was a dream that she was hearing. Detective Williams sat quietly listening to her cries. A knock at the door drew him back.

"Are you expecting anyone?" he asked. Alexis continued to weep. The detective walked to the door and answered it to see Malik standing there.

"Hello," Malik said, looking confused. "I'm here to see Alexis." He looked past the detective to see Alexis crying on the couch. He pushed past the detective and rushed to her side. "What's going on?" he asked.

The detective extended his hand to Malik. "I'm Detective Williams. You must be Ms. Thomas' father," he said.

Malik shook his hand and corrected him. "No. I'm her friend Malik."

The detective frowned and quickly fixed his face. He didn't want to get involved in her private affairs. *This man is old enough to be her,* daddy he thought to himself. "Well, I do apologize. Unfortunately, I had to deliver information to Ms. Thomas regarding someone she is associated with," the detective explained to Malik. "Ms. Thomas, I do apologize about you finding out in this manner. I want to give you time to get yourself together. But when you can, I need you to come and answer more questions for me. I'm going to leave my card on the table. Please call me as soon as you get the opportunity," he told her. "Have a good evening folks," he said as he walked out the door.

Malik walked behind him, locking the door. He had no clue as to what was going on. *All of this for a broken window?* he asked himself. Alexis sat with tears falling from her face. "What's wrong, princess?" he asked.

"He's dead," she said in a whisper.

"Who's dead?" Malik asked.

"He's gone," she said as she looked at Malik with heavy tears streaming from her face.

"Who is gone?" Malik asked, grabbing her hand. Seeing that she could not get the word out, Malik just held her close. "It's okay. Whatever it is, it's ok. Here, come with me. Let's get you out of here." Malik took Alexis by the hand and walked her to the front door. "Don't worry about anything. I'll take care of you," he told her.

He walked Alexis to his car and sat her in the passenger seat. He walked around to the driver's side. Starting the car, Malik reassured her that everything will be ok. "No worries. I got you a room downtown at the Four Seasons. I don't know what's going on, but I'm going to do the best I can to make you happy," he professed to her.

Alexis slowly turned and looked at him. There were so many emotions, she couldn't begin to describe. "You're married," she said in barely a whisper.

Malik's eyes grew large. "Wh-wh-what are you talking about?" he stuttered.

Alexis looked out the window as she watched the property security and maintenance board up her window until it could be replaced. "I know that you're married. I knew you were married when I first met you. You tried to lie and say that you weren't married, but I saw the band line on your ring finger. I know you're married," she reiterated.

Malik grew quiet for a second. He let out a large sigh and confessed. "Honestly, yes, I am married. My wife and I have been married now for about 12 years. Alexis, when I saw you, I didn't really think that I would get your phone number or hell, even get the opportunity to talk to you. My wife and I have been going through problems. Now I don't want to lie to you and tell you that we're going to get a divorce. I don't know if we will. Because of my career, she has the power to take away everything that I worked hard for. Don't get me wrong, I love my wife, but there are a lot of things that I've grown out of when it comes to her. When I met you, it was just something about you that drew me to you. I'm not saying that I'm trying to have a relationship. Right now, I just want to get to know you. I hope you can look past it. I know it sounds cliché, but I believe people are brought into your life for a reason. And I really want to get to know you more," he told her.

Alexis did not say anything and was quiet for a while. After a few more moments of silence she finally spoke. "Thank you for being honest with me," she said. She looked down at her phone and began playing with her message app. She saw that last text message from Collin and her eyes stung with tears.

"Do you want me to take you to the hotel?" he asked her.

"Yeah," she responded.

Malik started the car and drove out of the community towards downtown. The ride to the hotel was extremely quiet. Malik pulled into the parking lot and prepared to check her into the room. Alexis stopped him before he could open the door.

"Wait," she said as she grabbed his wrist. "Since you were honest with me, although I had to call you out on it, I guess I should be honest with you as well. Collin was my ex-boyfriend. He and I were together right before he died. We broke up over something that was my fault and now I feel like shit because of it," she cried.

Malik interlocked his fingers with hers and squeezed. "It's okay. I can't say that I know what it feels like to lose a loved one in that manner, but just know I'm here for whatever you need. And right now you need a friend." He wiped her tears and gave her a smile. "Now, I'm going to go check you into the hotel and get you settled in your room," he told her. "I'll be back in a few moments."

Alexis shook her head to let him know that she'd heard him and he got out of the car. Alexis looked at the cell phone and opened up her text messages again to see the last message that she'd received from Colin. She tried to understand why this happened to him but she couldn't. All she could hear were the detective's words ringing in her ears, telling her that his body was found. *Why didn't I just go up to him that day?* she asked herself as she thought about the day she saw him on campus with the pregnant girl. The thoughts ran through her mind as she waited for Malik to return. Almost as if she'd thought him up, he appeared, opening her door to help her out of the car.

"Okay, I got everything taken care of," he told her. "I'll walk you up to your room and get you settled in before I head out. Did you want me to get you something to eat?" he offered.

"No, I'm ok," she said. "I just want to lie down."

"Sure. I understand, princess." The two got in the elevator and proceeded to her room. Malik opened her door for her, letting her into the room.

Alexis looked around the room to see he'd booked the king suite. "Thank you," she told him. "I'm sorry that I brought all of this on you." She sat down on the edge of the bed and let out a sigh.

"Trust me, it's okay," he told her. "No need to apologize. At the end of the day, I'm glad I could help." He sat down next to her and rubbed her back. "Do you want to talk about it?" he asked her.

Alexis got quiet and just thought about the events of the day. "These last few months have just been crazy," she said.

"How so?" he asked her.

"Everything! Losing Collin, one of my best friends and I haven't spoken in almost 2 years. Right now, all I should be focused on is graduating from college but I have all of this other shit to deal with!" she said in frustration. "And here I am, telling everything to someone I barely know and pouring my heart out to a complete stranger," she told him.

"Hey, that's usually how it happens," he said with a smile. "But I understand. When you're going through a lot, it can be hard to talk to anybody. I can't do anything to stop the pain from you losing your ex-boyfriend. What I can do is offer to be here for you. As far as your best friend, well, one thing I can say about friendships is that if she's really your friend, she will understand and be there for you regardless. And if you're really her friend, you do what you can to make the friendship work," he told her.

Alexis listened to everything he was saying. "Funny. Everyone has been telling me the same thing," she said. Her mind kept going back to Collin. "I can't believe this is happening to me," she said. "Everyone that I love, I lose. Maybe I'm just meant to live this type of life."

Malik listened and wondered what she had experienced in her young life, and if he was really wanting to try to pursue anything with her. She seemed to have a lot of drama. *But she's fine as hell,* he thought. *What the hell is it about this girl?* He didn't know what it was about her but ever since he'd met her, he couldn't get her off his mind. He wanted to be there for her and help her in every way he could. And it didn't hurt that Alexis was drop dead gorgeous. Just being around her made him feel things he had not felt for his wife in quite some time. But he didn't want to rush her. He wanted to ask what she had really experienced, but decided against it. *She'll tell me when she's ready*, he thought.

He went into the bathroom to get her tissue. Coming back, he kissed her forehead. "I'm going to let you get some rest," he told her. "But you call me if you need anything."

Alexis sniffed and wiped her eyes. "Do you mind staying? It's been a lot of bad stuff today and right now, I just need someone to hold me," she requested.

"Sure; of course. I can stay for a few hours," he told her, quickly reminding her of his situation with her statement. Alexis agreed and lay on the bed. Malik lay on the bed next to her and placed in his arm around her. The two lay quietly for almost an hour. Malik relaxed to the rhythm of Alexis breathing. He adjusted himself on the bed to get comfortable, brushing his crotch against Alexis' backside. *Damn, her ass is nice*, he thought.

"Sorry about that," he said, as if she'd heard his thoughts.

Alexis felt his manhood against her backside. Although she was still hurting and upset, she needed some type of physical pleasure to make her forget the pain. She readjusted herself on the bed, making her ass brush against Malik's front. She knew this would make him want her. She turned to face him and looked him longingly in the eyes. She gave him a light kiss on the lips. Malik began to kiss her back while he sucked on her bottom lip. His hands caressed her lower back and ass. He grabbed a handful and squeezed, causing Alexis to moan in surprise. Alexis unbuckled his pants and placed her hand inside to feel his growing manhood. She was quite surprised at the size. He unzipped her jumpsuit jacket, exposing her breasts. He trailed kisses softly down her chest to her belly button and traced a circle with his tongue. Alexis let out a soft moan.

He got off the bed and took his shirt off, exposing his well-polished six pack. Alexis lay there admiring the sight. Malik bent over to grab her pants and pulled them down to her ankles, kissing and nipping at her thighs as he went. Alexis squirmed from the enjoyment. He pulled his pants off as if giving her a striptease. He climbed over her and began kissing her again.

"Are you sure you want to do this? If you don't, it's okay. I don't want to rush you."

Alexis answered him by kissing his lips and pulling him closer. He started kissing her lower body to taste her sweet nectar. He spread her lips and licked her clit slowly. Alexis' body felt as if it was going into convulsions. She dug her nails into his shoulders deeper and deeper as he tasted all of her.

"Yes!" she cried out in ecstasy. "Malik!" she whispered.

He flicked his tongue on and off of her clit, making her cum all over. Her body shuddered as if she had the chills. He sat up, looking down at her smiling as he pulled his now throbbing dick out of his briefs. He eased into her warm pussy. Alexis wrapped her legs around him, squeezing her lips on his dick as he slowly stroked in and out of her. He kissed her on her neck, sucking softly. Alexis' body was enjoying the pleasure Malik was giving her. She felt herself about to cum and squeezed her lips tighter. Alexis shuddered almost simultaneously with Malik. They kept going until five in the morning.

Alexis woke around 9am under the covers, hair disheveled and naked. She looked around and Malik was gone. She sat up and picked up her cell phone to check her messages. Realizing she had class in a few hours, she rushed to get dressed. She was about to call a cab when she noticed a note next to the phone.

Good morning Princess,

You were sleeping so quietly and I didn't want to wake you. My Town Car is downstairs for you when you are ready to head to class. He's been instructed to take you home to your car, no worries. I hope to hear from you, beautiful.

Malik

P.S. I still want Mimi's. ☺

Alexis smiled at the temporary happiness before she remembered the events from the night before. Grabbing her things, she decided it was time to make moves.

*

CHAPTER SEVEN

"Ladies and gentlemen! Introducing number 13 from Atlanta, Georgia, Alexis Thomas, known as RedRum!"

Alexis' new big sister pulled her face mask off and Alexis stepped out in front of the university. She looked into the stands to see it was packed with students coming to support their friends who had gone through the pledging process. She was beaming with pride as she had finally finished the process and was a Delta. She said her introductions, stepping back in line and waiting on her best friend to be introduced.

Moments later, she heard, "Ladies and gentlemen! Introducing number 21 from Tampa, Florida, Summer Alexander, known as Pulp Fiction!" The crowd went crazy in an uproar as Alexis watched her best friend step out and reveal herself to the University. Summer had a lot of friends excited for her.

Alexis scanned the crowd to see if Malik showed. He stood at one of the entrances of the gym smiling. Alexis smiled to herself as she knew later on he would be spoiling her with gifts. Her big sisters finished introducing the rest of the line and there probate ended.

Alexis ran over to Summer and the two grabbed each other, giggling and hugging while jumping up and down.

"We did it!" Summer said. "We're Deltas!"

"I can't believe it!" Alexis said.

At this point, all the students, faculty, and families were on the floor looking for the new initiates to congratulate. Alexis looked up and saw Tamika coming towards them. Tamika ran over to Summer and grabbed her.

"Oh my gosh, girl I'm so proud of you! Congratulations!" She turned to Alexis. "Congratulations as well, Alexis."

"Thank you," Alexis said. There was an awkward moment of silence between them.

"I can't believe you guys actually did it!" Tamika reiterated.

"Yep," Alexis said smiling. "We're Deltas!"

Tamika smiled at her ex-friend's enthusiasm. "Well, I won't hold you guys up," she said. "I just wanted to come and congratulate you both. Summer, I will hit you up later." She started to walk off and Alexis stopped her.

"Wait," she said. "I know we can't really talk right now. But how about tomorrow we all get up and go to lunch?" she said.

Tamika was caught by surprise. "Really?" she asked.

"Yeah," Alexis said. "I'll be the first one to admit that I've been a bit of a bitch these past couple of months. But now is really not the time to discuss that."

Tamika shook her head in agreement. "Yeah, you're right," she said "Okay, so I guess I will see you guys tomorrow. Summer, I will text you and you just let me know where to meet."

Alexis and Summer walked off to join their sisters in their celebrating.

"That was a shocker," Summer told her friend.

Alexis had been thinking about reconnecting with Tamika for a while but just didn't know how. "Yeah. I wasn't planning on saying anything to her. But I guess it was the perfect opportunity," Alexis said. "At the end of the day, it wasn't her fault. So I can at least hear her out. I don't know if we will be the best friends like we were before, but at the end of the day, I shouldn't hold it against her," she admitted.

"Damn!" Summer said. "If I'd have known that this would have been your reaction, I would have made you pledge a long time ago!" she laughed.

Alexis laughed as well. "Shut up, girl! Come on so we can go party," she said.

"I can definitely get with that," Summer agreed with her.

Alexis knew that with those letters, every man on campus would be trying to get at them. The Deltas were the hottest sorority on campus and everyone wanted to be one. But they only selected the chosen few. The two walked with their heads held high and all of the students in the area looked on. The girls could hear their new sisters doing the call and they quickly joined in.

*

Alexis and Summer sat at the restaurant waiting on Tamika. They'd decided to go to a restaurant that they all used to hang out. M&M Soul Food was right in the heart of campus and everyone loved to go there and enjoy the down home cooking. Alexis used to joke and say it was like The Pit from the television show *A Different World*. They ordered their drinks as Tamika walked through the door.

"Hey," she said. It seemed as if something was bothering her but Alexis was not going to be the one to ask.

"Hey," Alexis and Summer greeted. Tamika sat down as the waitress walked away. "We ordered you a sweet tea," Alexis told her.

"Okay, that's fine. Thank you," she said. "Okay, so do we want to dive right into this or do we want to eat first to me to ask?"

Alexis took a deep breath before she began to speak. "Well, I will say this. I wanted to apologize to you, too, Mika. I know that

151

you personally had nothing to do with what your brother did to me. I know it wasn't your fault. And I don't blame you for it. I don't know why I blamed you for it at the time. Honestly, I think it was just me being so frustrated with the entire situation and feeling as if no one was on my side. I'm so sorry if I hurt you." Alexis could feel the tears coming.

"That was not my intention. But it was so much anger that I had towards it all that I didn't know how to deal with. You should know that everyone told me that I was in the wrong but I was the one that wanted to be stubborn and not listen." She paused for a moment.

"I'm sorry for hanging up on you all of those times when you would call. I know that it must be difficult for you knowing that your brother is in prison and could even do something like that to one of your friends. I never stopped to think how it affected you. So before you say anything, I just wanted to let you know that I apologize to you. You have always been there for me since day one. And I never took that into consideration like I should have. I don't know if we will ever be best friends again, because there has been a lot that has been done as far as with certain members of your family. But what I do know is I'm not going to punish you for what they've done. I hope you are able to forgive me. Tamika, you are like my sister. And one thing I have learned within the last couple of months is that real friendships are hard to find."

Tamika sat listening to Alexis words and was very emotional. "Wow," she told Alexis. "I honestly wondered what I would say if you were to ever apologize, and I still have no words. I will say this; you are my sister. And I know what my brother did was really fucked up. And trust me, I really I hate the fact that we're related; especially now. But it wasn't as if I was on his side. It hurt me to know what he did to you. It hurt me to know what Keisha did to you."

Tamika held her head down and paused for a moment. "I tried to reach out to you, and at first I thought you just needed some space. But I'm sorry that I wasn't there for you. I should have been by your side. I let my own selfish thoughts and desires get in the way," she said apologetically.

Summer interjected. "What selfish thoughts and desires?" she asked. She had been followed the conversation up until now, but she was blindsided by what Tamika was referring to. Alexis looked at Tamika to see if she wanted to answer the question.

Tamika took a deep breath and responded. "Basically, during that timeframe that Alexis was attacked, a few nights before, I, uh, I tried to get at her," she said, avoiding eye contact. "I didn't know how to tell you, but I'm gay."

Summer sat back in amazement at what she was just told. "Really? Wow. And you knew this?" she asked Alexis.

Alexis nodded her head yes. "Yeah, I did. But it wasn't my place to tell. That's something she had to tell for herself."

Tamika jumped back on topic. "Well, again, I just wanted to let you know that I'm sorry for not being there for you. I know it's been really hard for you lately. Everyone is talking about Collin's death." Tamika stopped talking, unsure of how Alexis would react. She could tell Alexis was saddened. "There's something else," Tamika said.

"Tamika, what is wrong with you?" Summer asked?

Tamika's entire expression changed. "I don't know how to tell you guys this."

"Tell us what?" Alexis asked.

Tamika took a sip of her drink and put it back down on the table. "I got a phone call from Fayetteville Hoke County Correctional Institute."

Alexis immediately frowned, as she knew that was where Jayshawn was currently serving time. "Okay, so what? Is his sentence being shortened or something?" Alexis asked. "Or better yet, did the nigga die?"

Summer looked at Alexis with a concerned face. "Alexis, calm down. Tamika, what's going on?" She asked.

Tamika swallowed and told her, "I got a phone call from the prison saying that Jayshawn had managed to escape. No one knows where he is right now. They checked his cell but there was nothing in there to indicate that he was escaping."

Alexis' nerves were on edge. "Are you fucking kidding me right now? This nigga can be here in Greensboro and I don't even know it," she said. "How did they know for sure that he is gone?"

Tamika told her the information the warden told her. "Apparently he was on laundry duty or something at the prison, and they believe he may have escaped in a large round of laundry that was shipped out for cleaning for the guards," she said. "They checked all the areas but there is not so much as a hint to give them an idea as to where he is. They are pretty sure that he's here in Greensboro. It's just a matter of where he is."

Summer was worried for her friend Alexis. "Well, did he contact you?" she asked. "Did he say anything?"

Alexis looked at Tamika for a response.

"No. He wrote me one letter when he was in prison and I wrote him back saying that I never wanted to hear from him because of what he did. I told him to leave me the hell alone. I let him know that he needed to rot in prison," she said with conviction.

Alexis slowed her breathing to calm down. "So that means he can be anywhere right now. Wait a minute. How long ago did he escape?" she asked.

Tamika told her that she checked her voicemail two days ago. She had to check her voicemail to get the information. Tamika had always been one that would have over 15 voicemails before she checked them all, so they could be important messages that sat in her inbox for weeks at a time.

"How long has he been out?" Alexis asked.

"For about a month and a half," Tamika answered her.

"Shit." Alexis looked at Summer. "You don't think that he killed Collin, do you?" Alexis asked in a panic. "I mean, that detective did say that he died of a gunshot wound to the back of the head. What if he did this? What if he did this to get to me? What if he's coming for me?" Alexis asked, her voice full of fear.

Summer grabbed Alexis. "Girl, calm down," she told her.

"I can't calm down!" Alexis yelled. "I can't calm down because the muthafucka that damn near killed my ass is free. He managed to escape from prison, Summer! That's not some fuckin boot camp. He escaped from prison. And for all I know he's coming for me right now," she told her.

"Well, he has to get through us," Tamika said.

"I got to get the hell out of here," Alexis said. She pulled her phone out and sent a text message to Malik.

Alexis: Hey baby. I need your help. It's an emergency.

Malik was at work but she knew he would respond.

"Who are you calling?" Summer asked.

"I gotta come up with some money to get out of here fast," Alexis explained to her.

"Alexis, I really think you should call the cops first rather than that dude. Besides, they know that he's escaped so I'm sure they're looking for him," Summer said.

"You don't understand. That nigga tortured me in that closet. I can't let him find me," she urged.

"He won't get to you. If we need to, we will stay with you," Tamika suggested.

"Yeah," Summer said in agreement. "We'll be with you when you go to class and be with you every step of the way. Seriously, Lex. You're this close to graduating. We have three weeks left. And then we walk across the stage," she said.

"That's true. And I know that you've worked hard to graduate. Even with everything that's happened, you're still graduating on time," Tamika told her in amazement.

"Damn, I need to get on your education plan, bitch," Summer said, joking. "You took a semester off and still managed to graduate on time," she said with a light laugh to lighten up the mood.

Alexis heard her but all she could think about was Jayshawn coming to look for her. She was scared because she knew there was a possibility that he would be successful.

Tamika looked at Alexis and saw her hands were shaking. "Are you okay?"

She shook her head. "No," she responded. "Why won't this shit fuckin stop?" she asked. "I just want to live a normal life!" Alexis was starting to get upset and was drawing attention from other customers.

"Let's just go and we'll figure something out." Tamika looked at Alexis and promised her that she wouldn't let what happened last time happen again. They decided to go to Alexis' house. Tamika followed in her car.

Alexis drove down the highway with her mind racing. "I can't keep running, Summer. Alexis said. "I can't keep living my life like this," she spoke out loud.

Summer didn't interrupt, as she figured her friend needed this time to vent. When she was finished, she told her, "Like I said, Alexis, just let the police handle it."

"For what?" Alexis asked. "Obviously if the police were handling it, he wouldn't be out of prison now. If the police were handling it, he would have been in a maximum security facility. Instead of some damn Fayetteville prison where clearly, they don't pay attention to their inmates, otherwise he wouldn't have escaped."

"I understand all of that," Summer calmly said to her friend. "But right now, the best thing for us to do is it just stick together. He can't come at all of us. You have a gun, right?" she asked her.

"Oh, hell yes!" Alexis answered. "I have several guns. I'm not going down without a fight this time," she told her. "He wants me, he's going to get me. But not in the way that he thinks." As she gripped the steering wheel, she was determined and hell-bent on making sure that she wouldn't let him control her any more than he already had. *He may have caught me off guard*, she thought to herself, *but best believe that's the last time.*

*

CHAPTER EIGHT

The three pulled up to Alexis' house and walked inside. "Do you really think it's wise to stay here, though?" Tamika asked. "I mean, even though you moved, with everything that has happened here already, from what you told me, who's to say that it's not him and that he doesn't already know where you live?" she asked.

Alexis thought about what her friend said. "That's true. But I will be damned if I have someone run me out of my own house."

"Well, whatever you decide to do, you know we got your back," Summer told her.

"Right," Tamika agreed. She thought of something Alexis had said earlier. "You said you thought I was calling you from a bunch of unknown numbers?" she asked, concerned.

"Yea." Alexis responded. "It wasn't you?"

Tamika shook her head no. Alexis now assumed that it was him trying to get to her. Her phone buzzed and she looked to see Malik's response.

Malik: What's up, princess? On my way to the courthouse for afternoon session.

She decided to take Summer's advice. She would call the cops first and if they couldn't do anything then she would reach out to Malik.

Alexis: Nvm baby. I've got it handled.

Malik responded within a few seconds. She knew he always made her a priority.

Malik: Ok princess. I'll call you in a few.

Alexis was about to put her phone up when she saw the detective's number at the bottom of her purse. She pulled the card out, calling the number that was listed.

"Williams," he answered on the second ring.

"Detective Williams? This is Alexis Thomas. I think I may have information that may help regarding Collin's death. Well, at least I think so," she told him.

"I'm listening," Detective Williams said.

Alexis prepared to tell him the newfound information. "Well, two years ago, I was kidnapped by my next door neighbor and his girlfriend, who was my ex-boyfriend's baby mama. His sister goes to school with me and is one of my good friends. Long story short, they tortured me."

The detective's head was spinning from what she told him. "Okay let me make sure I heard this correctly," Detective William stated. "You're best friends to someone that is related to a person that attacked you? The boyfriend that you had was the baby daddy to the girlfriend of the offender?" he verified.

"Correct," she said. "But the reason why I'm calling is because the guy, Jayshawn Cheston, has escaped from prison and I think he may have been the one that killed Collin," she said, scared.

"Ok. I do believe I remember reading something about an inmate escaping in our emails. This will be handled immediately. In the meantime, I would suggest that you stay out of sight for a while. Don't worry," he told her. "Typically when an inmate escapes, they go back to what is familiar to them and we pick them up within a few weeks. So we'll have officers patrol his old home, work and anywhere else that he was associated."

"Ok," she said, thankful that she had moved out of the complex. "Thanks for your help." She ended the call. She sent a text message to Henderson to let him know what was going on.

Alexis: Hey, sorry to bother. I just found out that Jayshawn escaped from prison. Don't know for sure if he is in G-boro but, I figured u would wanna know.

Henderson: R u ok?

Alexis: Yea. Summer & Tamika are here with me.

Henderson: Word? Mika's there?

Alexis: Yea. We're good. Tell u about it later.

Henderson: Do u need me to come down there?

Alexis: No I should be ok. Besides, I can't put u at risk and u got Ti Ti.

Henderson: Aight but just remember what I taught u. Keep them burners loaded and ready. Aim straight if u gotta use it.

Alexis: I remember. I'll text u later.

Henderson: Aight.

Alexis saw that it was after four o'clock and decided to ask Malik for some help. She sent him a quick text.

Alexis: Hey sweetie, I have a little bit of a situation. We need to talk. Can we meet at our usual spot?

Ever since the night Malik took her to that hotel, they had been meeting there at least once a week to spend time together. He didn't want to risk his wife or any of their friends seeing them together and Alexis was okay with that. He would come to the room and she would already be inside waiting for him. They had the perfect relationship because she gave him what he needed, attention, and he gave her anything she asked for. She became his princess. He responded a few minutes later.

Malik: I won't be able to meet you until about 6 o'clock. Is that okay?

Alexis: Yeah that's fine. I have to run some errands and then I'll meet you there.

She had planned on asking Malik to get her an apartment in his name but no one would know the location. She knew that it might be doing a little bit too much, but she didn't feel safe in her home.

"Or you can stay on campus with me," she heard Summer say.

"I'm sorry; what?" Alexis asked.

"Damn, girl, where were you just now?" Summer asked.

Alexis just shook her head. "Girl, don't worry about it," she said. "My mind is all over the place right now."

"Well that's why Summer was suggesting you stay with her on campus. That way you would be around a lot of people at one time. And you never have to worry about being by yourself," Tamika filled her in.

"I can't do that," Alexis told her. "Security isn't tight enough on campus. Didn't one of the dorms get hit a few weeks ago? He can easily blend in as a student. Y'all think about it," she told them.

"Well, what do you want to do?" Tamika asked.

"I'm going to stay here in my house," Alexis told her. She did not, however, tell her the plans that she had to get a secret apartment. The less they knew, the less they were at risk. Plus, Alexis knew Summer didn't like her sleeping with a married man for money.

"Ok," Summer said. "Well then we're here with you."

"Thanks, y'all," Alexis said, smiling for the first time since she'd found everything out. "I appreciate it."

"Girl, bye. That's what we're here for. You don't have to thank us for that. We're your friends." Tamika told her. "I'm going to run to my house and grab some stuff so that way I'm not driving back and forth. I'll be back in about an hour or so. Are y'all going to be good?"

"Yeah, we should be fine," Alexis told her. "Go ahead and handle your business."

"Ok, I'll hit you up when I'm on the way back." Tamika walked out the door, leaving Summer and Alexis in the condo.

"So are you going to tell your dad?" Summer asked her.

"Not yet," Alexis said. "My thing is they called Tamika and let her know. How come no one has contacted me? Don't you think they should contact the victim to let them know that the person that raped and hurt them is now on the run? I haven't gotten so much as a phone call."

"But didn't you change your number?" Summer asked?

"Yeah. But they should still be able to contact me. And if they can't contact me, they can contact my father. My father hasn't said anything to me and I just talked to him yesterday," she explained.

"Yeah, but your dad hardly ever checks his cell phone."

No sooner than Summer said than Alexis' phone began to ring and she saw her father's name on the caller ID. Alexis quickly picked it up.

"Hey, dad."

"Alexis!" her dad yelled. "Where are you? Are you okay? I've been trying to reach you!"

"Calm down, Daddy," she said. "I'm fine. I already know. Tamika told me that Jayshawn escaped from prison. They haven't confirmed whether or not he's here. I didn't get any notification from the prison or the warden. But I'm ok. Summer is here with me now."

"No," he said. "That's not going to work. You need to get your butt on a plane, or get in your car. Right now!"

"Daddy, are you serious?" Alexis asked. "We have three weeks left until graduation. If I leave now, I'm going to miss finals and I won't be able to graduate," she told him. "Trust me, daddy, I'm fine. Nobody can get into the condo without one of the guards letting them in. The only way they'll do that is if you're on the approved list. Plus, I still have exams. Summer and Tamika are going to stay at the condo with me. They will always be with me. I just don't want to risk leaving and not be able to graduate. I missed a whole semester already. I won't miss anymore school because of him," she said strongly.

"That was my whole point of coming to North Carolina, to go to school and get my degree. I'm not going to let him stop me, Daddy. I know you worry, and I understand. But trust me. I can handle myself," she tried to reassure her father.

"Well then, I'm coming there," her father told her.

"What?" She said. "Daddy, that's really not necessary."

"Alexis, I don't care. I'm not just going to let you sit while some man is out there trying to hurt you. I'm not going to lose my daughter, and that's that," he said.

"Daddy, please. It's hard enough as is trying to concentrate and get ready for graduation. It's not going to make the situation better if you're here. If anything, it'll make it worse. Not saying you irritate me, but I would be worried about you and not be able to focus on school." She paused. "I tell you what. What if I stayed with Uncle Brandon?"

Her father's brother was a police officer in High Point, which was about 25 minutes away from Alexis. "I can call him and ask him can I stay with them until graduation. That way I know I'm protected. And besides, I carry my gun with me everywhere," she told him.

Her father got quiet and thought about her proposition. "You promise me that you're going to be careful and you will call me every day?" he asked.

"Yes, Daddy, I will be," she said. "I promise I will make sure that I don't put myself in any situation where I could be harmed. And if I even think it's getting dangerous, I will be getting in my car and headed straight to Atlanta," she told him.

"Ok. But I'm serious, baby girl. You gotta be careful. No ripping and running. And the first day I don't hear from you, I'm coming," he told her.

"I know, Daddy. I will," she said. "I love you."

"I love you, too, baby," he told her before he hung up the phone.

Summer sat on the couch waiting for Alexis to finish our conversation. "So everything is cool?" she asked.

"Yeah, it's straight," Alexis told her. "He wanted me to come home but I told him to let me stay at least through graduation. That way I'm not messing up my walking."

"Oh, ok. That's what's up. We need something to get our minds off this mess. If you want, tonight we can go to that new club downtown, the Empire Room. My friend told me it's popping. And ladies are free before midnight," Summer tried to persuade Alexis.

"I don't know. I'm not really in the mindset to party right now," Alexis said. "I'm going to start packing up some of my stuff tonight. We can do a girls' night in, though," Alexis suggested.

"Ok, cool!" Summer said. "When Tamika gets back, I'll go ahead and go to the store and stock up on junk food. But you know I gotta go to the ABC store. Gotta get my brown!"

Alexis laughed at her friend. "I swear, you love that Hennessy. But hey, do you," she said "Well, while you go to the ABC store, I'm going to go to my counseling session," she lied. She figured she could meet Malik at the hotel while Summer was out getting everything for girls' night.

She looked to see Summer's hesitancy. "Relax. It's not like you can come in there with me anyway. It's a private session. At most, you would just be sitting in the car anyway so why not go ahead and get everything then? That way we can all come back to the house and not have to do anything else," she said. She did plan on stopping at her session but that was to get her clearance paperwork which would only take a few minutes.

"I guess," Summer told her. "So, what I will do is get everything and then come sit in the parking lot and wait," she informed her.

"Ok, cool." Alexis looked at the clock to see that it was 5:15. She'd told Malik that she would meet him at the hotel at 6 p.m. "Alright, let me go ahead and grab my stuff and we can go," she told Summer.

Setting the house alarm, she and Summer walked out the door. Alexis dropped Summer off to her car and drove off to meet Malik.

*

Tamika walked into her apartment building texting on her phone. Looking down the entire time, she saw Summer had texted her to let her know they were going to do a girls' night in. She was responding to the message when his voice called out of her.

"Hey, sis," he said calmly. Tamika looked to see Jayshawn sitting at her dining room table.

"Jayshawn, what the hell are you doing here? Why did you come here?" Tamika asked.

"No worries. There'll be time for questions later," he told her, ordering her to sit on the couch.

Tamika kept her eyes on her brother the entire time. "What are you doing? You got to go," she told him.

"So you didn't want talk to me, huh? Support your brother while he was in jail?" he asked.

"Are you serious, Shawn? Do you know what you did to our family?" she cried. "Please, Sean, just go. I promise, I won't say anything."

Jayshawn looked at his sister crying and laughed. "Oh, you mad I tried to kill the bitch you've been tryna fuck?" he asked. "You so concerned about the family. Does the family know you're a dyke?"

Her eyes grew large and she got quiet.

"Yeah that's what I thought," he said.

Tamika looked at him, pleading. "What are you going to do?" she asked. When she saw him pull out a silencer, she crumbled. "Jayshawn... I'm your sister," she told him. "Remember?"

"Like you said, you're only my half-sister." He raised his gun and, before she could get a scream out, a single bullet went through her heart. "See you later, sis," he said. He grabbed her cell phone and handbag and walked out the door. "One down, one to go," he said.

*

171

Ariane woke up to find the bed empty. She had been sleeping a lot more since she was in her last trimester and was due any day. She looked at her phone to see that it was after midnight. Her brother had gotten an apartment in his name for Jayshawn to stay and lay low. Since he couldn't really go too far without getting caught, she had been staying there to get what he needed. She would come over and clean up and cook for him and do whatever else he needed her to do. He told her that as soon as he finished his business that they would be leaving to go to Atlanta. She wanted to help him, but because of the fact that she was so big, she could barely get out the bed.

She decided to text him to see where he was. Before she could hit the send button, she heard the keys in the lock of the front door. Jayshawn walked in, throwing his keys down on the table.

"Hey," he said, not even looking at her.

"Hey, babe," she responded. "Everything okay?" She noticed that he had some blood on his pants but didn't want to question him. He had been very moody lately but she figured it was because he was nervous about the baby.

"Yeah I'm straight," he told her. "You been laying in the bed all day?" he asked.

"Yeah," she said, a little uneasy. "The baby has been really active today so it made me a little tired."

"Yeah, whatever," he told her. "I'm hungry. Go fix me something to eat," he demanded.

Ariane walked to the kitchen to fix him food. "What do you want?" she asked.

"Damn, do I got to do everything?" he asked her. "Just pick something, damn!"

Ariane quietly went into the kitchen and looked in the cabinet. "I got to go to the store," she said. She was hoping he would tell her not to worry about it because it was late. Instead, he walked to the bedroom, slamming the door behind him.

Sighing, Ariane walked over to the front door, put her shoes on and walked down the steps to head to the store. Her back began to bother her as she walked to the car. She felt a sharp pain in her side. Her body was still sore from scrubbing the floors earlier. Jayshawn had asked her to clean up the house and he was very meticulous when it came to his stuff.

She got in cranking her car and a few seconds later felt another pain.

"Oh shit," she said to herself. "I can't be in labor yet."

She picked up her phone and called Jayshawn. His phone continuously rang and after so many rings, it went to voicemail. She hit the redial button to try him again, thinking that he had stepped away from his phone for a minute. When she got no answer again and the pain became more intense, she decided to drive herself to the hospital. Hopefully, he would meet her there. She called the hospital to let them know that she was on the way. She sent Jayshawn a text message letting him know that she was not going to the store and to ask if he could meet her at the hospital. When she arrived, the nurses were waiting for her to be admitted. She checked in and they took her straight to the labor and delivery room. They begin to hook her up to the machines and her contractions became more severe.

"I'm not having this baby until he gets here," she said to the nurses in the room all rushing.

One of the nurses looked at her concerned. "Ma'am, we have to act quickly. Your baby is in danger," she told her.

Ariane's face looked fearful. "What do you mean, danger? I just had a doctor's appointment two days ago and she said that everything was fine."

Then nurse looked at Ariane and gave her the news. "I'm sorry, but you are at risk of losing this baby. The heartbeat is not as strong as it should be, and it looks as if there is some trauma. We're going to do what we can, but we need to do an emergency C-section," she explained.

Ariane was scared because nothing was going to plan. She was excited about her baby and the opportunity for Jayshawn and her to be a family. She had written out the birth plan that the Lamaze coaches suggested. She even picked a focus object. She was excited because Jayshawn would be there to experience it with her. Hearing them tell her that she had to have an emergency C-section made her nervous and scared. But she would do anything to save her baby; even if it meant having it alone.

"Okay now we're going to go ahead and take you to the operating room. The anesthesiologist is going to give you this spinal, which is going to make you numb from the neck down. This will make it easier for us to cut you open and get the baby out. You want to make sure that you do not move because the slightest movement could cause a risk of paralysis. It may make you a little groggy or nauseous, so we're going to stick a patch behind your ear to prevent that. Do you have any questions?" the nurse asked as they wheeled her down the hall.

Ariane thought about the welfare of her baby. "No," she whispered. She remembered that Jayshawn had not responded. "I need to call my boyfriend and let him know that I'm at the hospital," she said.

"I'm sorry, but at this point we can't waste any more time," the nurse informed her.

The monitors that were hooked up to Ariane's stomach begin to beep at an increasing rate. "Pressure is dropping!" she heard one of the nurses yell. "Let's get a move on!"

They arrived at the operating room and Ariane lay with her heart racing. She closed her eyes so that she could not physically see what was going on. She was so scared. The doctor put a sheet on top of her stomach and began to operate. Ariane lay unable to see what was going on below her body. She felt pressure from the doctor moving her hands. After about twenty minutes, she felt the pressure stop as the doctor removed the baby.

Ariane held her head up to see what was going on. "What's happening? Is it a boy or girl?" she asked. She looked to see one of the nurses hold her head down solemnly and walk the baby out the room. Immediately, her guard was raised. "What's wrong with my baby? Why can't I see my baby?" she asked.

The doctor turned to Ariane. "I'm sorry, but the baby…she didn't make it. It looks like there wasn't enough oxygen to the brain," the doctor explained.

Ariane shook her head slowly. "No," she said. "She was just moving!" she explained to the doctor.

Before she knew it, she had lost consciousness.

*

Jayshawn lay on the bed rolling a blunt. He'd heard Ariane leave a while ago to go to the store. *What the fuck is taking her so long?* he thought to himself. He picked up the phone she had bought him to call her. He saw that he had a few missed calls from her and text messages. The last message he received told him that she was in labor and on her way to the hospital. *I hope she doesn't think I'm coming up in that muthafucka,* he thought to himself. *I'm not about to put my fuckin plan at risk because this bitch went and had a baby.* He put the phone back on his nightstand.

Getting up, he decided to fix him something himself. When he saw that there was nothing in the pantry, he grabbed his keys and decided to go grab something. He had been out for a few months and was staying close to his apartment. Ariane's brother had gotten him a fake I.D., an apartment and hit him up with some furniture. He drove up to Charlotte to meet with Meech to get the loan so he could get started hustling. He automatically stashed half of it in an account under a fake name and used the other half to get himself straight and get back in the game.

He picked up the phone that he had taken from Tamika when he was at her apartment. He looked in it to find Alexis' new number and decided to have some fun. Blocking her number, he called her as private. As tempted as he was to leave her a voicemail, he decided against it. He planned on getting an address from her soon. He was almost certain that at this point she was aware he was out of prison.

His phone began ringing again and saw Ariane was calling him again. He didn't want to talk and opted to send her a text message.

Jayshawn: What?

Ariane: I need you. Where you at?

Jayshawn: I'm chillin.

Ariane: I lost the baby. Please just come up here.

Jayshawn: Can't risk being caught.

Ariane: Maybe you didn't hear me say I lost the baby?

Jayshawn was starting to get irritated with her.

Jayshawn: Ok. I saw that. What you want me to do? It ain't gonna change nuthin.

Ariane: Really Shawn? Is that how you want to act? After everything I've done for you.

Jayshawn laughed at her message and knew he was pissing her off.

Jayshawn: And what have you done for me lately besides slow me down? I told you I'm not trying to have no baby right now.

After a few minutes of no response, Jayshawn smirked and continue to roll up a blunt.

*

Ariane was furious. She had had enough of Jayshawn treating her like shit. Hurt by the loss of her baby and knowing that Jayshawn would never change, she broke down. She cried so hard it was difficult for her to breathe. The nurses in the room thought she was upset over the baby, but it was so much more than that. Ariane felt like she wanted to die. She didn't know how much more she could take.

All of this for him, she thought to herself. I put myself and my baby at risk just to get him out. And this is how he treats me? I lost my baby and it's all his fault. Why do I keep letting him do this to me? Ariane promised herself and her child that she would make sure Jayshawn paid for hurting her. All of this time, she thought. All this time, and he played me.

"It's not fair!" she said out loud.

One nurse came over and gave her a tissue and held her hand. "I know, sweetie. I know it's not fair. Do you have anybody that we can call?" she asked. Ariane saw her name was Nurse Jill Martin.

"No. I don't. My baby daddy acting like he doesn't want to come up here. He's made me lose everybody. My family doesn't want anything to do with me, and now I lost my baby. What am I going to do?" she asked.

The nurse felt sorry for her. She looks so young, she thought to herself. This poor girl has been through it all.

"One thing you can do now is pray. That's what I tell myself when things get rough," she said.

"I feel like I just want to die," Ariane told her.

"Never feel like you want to die. Your spirit is broken, but it's not gone, baby. I'm your nurse on duty tonight, Nurse Jill Martin. Do you want me to stay with you?" she asked her.

"Yes, please," Ariane answered.

The nurse sat praying, holding her hand. She didn't know that Ariane vowed to herself she would get revenge for the damage that had been done.

*

Ariane awoke to find herself in a hospital room alone. She saw flowers sitting on her food tray. Thinking they were from Jayshawn, she read the card. "No matter what, you are loved. Always keep God first." She remembered then why she was there. What hurt her more than anything was that Jayshawn was not there for her.

We should be one happy family right now, she thought to herself. I should be holding my child in my arms and looking down at her telling her how beautiful she is. Instead, he's somewhere probably getting high. I did everything for him, she thought to herself.

"Well, no more. If this is what he wants to do," she said out loud, "then I don't need him. I deserve better, and I will get better." She thought about every possible way that she could get revenge on Jayshawn. An idea came to mind and she wiped her tears, replacing it with an evil smile. She now needed the two people she'd hated the most and planned to eliminate.

"I know just what to do," she said out loud. She called Alexis' number. She had called it multiple times before, blocking her phone number so that Alexis wouldn't know who it was. *Hopefully she answers,* she thought to herself. The phone rang another three rings.

"Hello?" the girl finally answered.

"Hi. Alexis, you don't know me. But I have very important information regarding the man that you put in prison. Jayshawn is my ex-boyfriend. He's been sending me death threats and saying that he was going to kill me. He killed some guy a couple of weeks ago. The news reporter was saying that they thought it was your boyfriend. I'm scared and don't want to talk over the phone. Do you think that we could meet soon?"

Ariane was putting on the performance of a lifetime with tears and all.

"Wait, what?" Alexis inquired. "How do I know this isn't a trick? Better question is how do you know he did it?"

"Believe me," she said convincingly, "it's not. I understand that you may be nervous or scared. But I'm just as scared."

"Then why are you calling me private?" Alexis asked.

"Because I'm not using my phone," Ariane answered quickly. "Look, I just thought that we could talk because your life is in danger just as much as mine. He's crazy. He kept saying you gotta pay. Look, I'm going to be at Barber Park tomorrow around 6 p.m. Please just meet me there. I know you don't know me, but there are a lot of things that you need to know," Ariane pleaded with her.

She knew that the way she played that role, Alexis would show. "I'll think about it," Alexis responded after a few minutes. "If I show up, I show up. But don't think that you can try to pull one over on me. Don't try no funny shit. Or you will get fucked up."

Yeah right, bitch, Ariane thought to herself, reassuring Alexis on the phone that there was no danger in meeting her before hanging up. She planned on putting the second part of her plan into play the minute she was released from the hospital. At that moment, Nurse Jill walked into the room.

"Hey. I just wanted to come and check on you. You were asleep for a really long time. We gave you some meds to help you relax," she explained.

"Thank you," she told the nurse. The nurse reminded her of her mother before she'd put her out for being with Jayshawn.

"It's no problem, honey. How you feeling?" she asked.

"I'm okay, I guess. I just want to go home."

"Well, physically, you're fine to go home. You can go home as early as tonight if you'd like. But I would suggest staying one more day so that you can get your mind together," Nurse Jill suggested.

"No, I will be ok," she told her. "Besides, I've been talking with the pastor at my church and he said that he can help me," Ariane lied.

"Ain't God good?" The nurse smiled.

Ariane felt a twinge of guilt for lying to her. She had been nothing but nice to her since she'd gotten there but she didn't want anyone to try to talk her out of what she needed to do.

"Yea, He is. Tell you what. I will stay until tomorrow morning. That way, you don't have to worry about me," Ariane suggested.

The nurse smiled. "I will be just fine with that, baby," she said, patting her hand. "And I am going to leave you my number. You can call me at any time. Now, let's get you fed," she said as she picked up the menu for Ariane to look over.

Ariane sat back and let the nurse take care of her. She had been doing for everyone else, so even if for a brief moment, she was going to enjoy it.

*

183

CHAPTER NINE

Alexis and Summer were sitting at her apartment watching TV waiting on Tamika to come back when Ariane had called. Alexis finished her conversation.

"Who the hell was that?" Summer asked.

"Some chic Jayshawn used to date named Ariane," Alexis told her.

"And you're just supposed to believe that?" Summer asked agitated.

"No," Alexis said. "But she did have a lot of information. She wants me to meet her tomorrow at Barber Park at 6 o'clock."

"Lex, I really hope that you're not going to do this. Maybe you should call your dad. Or hell, call that detective you said came by," Summer suggested.

"I can't do that," Alexis told her. "You know he would overreact. Besides, I've gone through too much with this muthafucka and I am not going to let him win," She spat.

"Okay, but how do you know that she's not working with him?" Summer asked her skeptically. "For all you know, this could be a setup to get you out to some location and get rid of you or some shit."

"I feel you," Alexis explained. "But at the same time, you and Mika will be there so I won't be by myself."

Summer had a bad feeling about it. "I don't know, Lex. I mean, something just don't seem right about this. Like, I mean, she just literally popped up out nowhere. I don't trust her and I don't think you should go. Like I said before, I think you should call that detective."

"Yeah, but it may not be anything. I wanna find out for myself first," Alexis said. "I don't wanna get my father worked up and bothered unless it's absolutely necessary. And like I said, you and Mika can go with me and we can get there early. Speaking of Tamika, I wonder where she is and why she didn't call or text us to let us know she wasn't coming back," Alexis said, changing the subject.

"I don't know," Summer said. "That's not like her, though. I'm going to go try to call her again," she said. She walked off into the room to go get her cell phone.

Alexis' phone began to vibrate and she saw that it was a private number. *Maybe it's Tamika*, she thought. She picked it up and answered.

"Hello?" She heard someone breathing on the other end. For some reason, she knew it was Jayshawn. "I know it's you, muthafucka. Hear me and hear me good. I am not scared of you. You, on the other hand, should be scared. Cause the cops will find your ass, bitch. That's why your ass is calling me from a fuckin blocked number. You better hope that I don't see you. Cause I'm ready for you this time. Don't fuck with me!" she said before hanging up the phone.

"Girl, who the hell are you talking to?" Summer asked as she walked back into the room.

"Nobody girl," she said dismissing it so that Summer wouldn't question her. The last thing she wanted to hear was Summer's mouth if she knew she was on the phone with him. "So what did Tamika say?" she asked, changing the subject.

"She didn't answer," Summer said. "I called her mom and she said that she hadn't heard from her but, when she gets off work, she's going to go by her house to check and see if maybe she's asleep or something. She told me she was worried about her because she hadn't really been going to sleep lately."

"Damn. Well, hopefully, I guess we'll see her tomorrow. Speaking of sleep, I'm bout to take my ass to bed, girl. I'm tired," Alexis said, yawning. "I put some towels and stuff in the room for you." Summer was staying in the spare bedroom. "Let me know if you need anything. I'm bout to lay it down."

"Are you okay?" Summer asked.

"Yeah, girl, I'm fine," Alexis answered, reassuring her.

"Okay, just making sure," Summer said to her friend.

"Alright, I'll see you in the morning. Come on, Chubs," She called her dog and he followed her into the room. Alexis closed her bedroom door and climbed into her bed. She was on her way to sleep when she heard her phone ringing and saw Malik was calling her. She made sure to put on her sexiest voice.

"Hey, baby," she answered.

"Hey, princess," he said, tired. "How are you?"

"I'm good," she answered. "Just getting in the bed getting ready to go to sleep. Got a few tests tomorrow. It's almost that time," she told him.

"Oh, I know, princess," he said. "I just wanted to give you a call. I've been thinking about you."

"Oh really?" she asked. "And what has my sexy daddy been thinking?"

"I been thinking about how much I miss you. I hate that I can't see you right now," he confessed, turning her on with his deep voice.

"Aw, baby, I miss you, too," she said. "But don't worry; you know I can't wait to see you. Where are you right now? I'm surprised that she's not fussing at you for calling so late."

"I'm in the office. I swear the life of a criminal defense attorney is never easy. I wish you could be with me right now," he answered, getting serious.

"I understand, baby. I wish I could be there with you right now," she purred.

"Me, too. I'm in the office not wanting to go home. You know I wish I could be at your graduation, right?" he asked her.

"I know," she told him. "But you know my father will be there and I don't think he would take too well to me dating a married man," she suggested. Malik got quiet on the phone at her comment. "Are you still there?" she asked.

She heard Malik let out a sigh. "I've been wanting to talk to you about that. I'm leaving her. I filed for divorce from my wife. Alexis, you've known that I wasn't happy for quite some time. And nobody makes me feel the way you do. So I'm leaving her. I want to be with you. I know that right now we can't really be seen together except in hidden locations, but you make me feel things that I have not felt in a while. You make me happy. You know exactly what to do. And that's what I need," he told her.

Alexis was taken aback by everything she heard. "Wow," she said. "I don't know what to say, baby," she told him. "That was a lot that you just sprung on me." Alexis truly was in shock after hearing what Malik had just told her. She knew that she had been satisfying him but not to the point where he would want to leave his wife and family.

"How is it surprising that I love you?" he asked, interrupting her thoughts.

"No, I'm not saying you don't," Alexis responded. "I just thought that we were just kind of taking it light. You know I love you, too. I just don't want you to put everything at risk for me," she told him, playing the concerned role. She knew that she had no intentions of being with him long term, or it being anything other than a financial relationship.

"Trust me, baby, I'm not putting anything at risk when it comes to you," she heard him say. "I deserve to be with someone that is going to make me happy, and that's you. Don't you want to be with me?" he asked her. "Cause I'm not trying to force you to be with someone you don't wanna be with, or do something you don't want to do."

"Of course I want to be with you!" she told him. "That goes without question," she lied. "I'm sorry, I wasn't trying to make you think I did not want to be with you. It's just with everything going

190

on for graduation, that's been my main focus, so it just caught me off guard," she said trying to recover.

"Oh, ok. I can definitely understand that," he told her. "How about after graduation I take you away for a week? We can go anywhere you want to go."

"Really?" she asked. "Are you sure you can be gone that long without your wife getting suspicious?"

"Trust me, since the divorce papers were filed, she hardly has said two words to me. Besides," he told her, "I don't care what she has to say. You just tell me where you want to go and I will make it happen."

Alexis decided to pick someplace exotic and out of the country, thinking he would not be able to make it happen. "Ok," she told him. "I want to go to Anguilla. I've always dreamed of going there."

"Anguilla, huh?" he asked her.

"Yep," she said.

"Well, then Anguilla it is," he responded.

"Really?" Alexis asked, excited and intrigued.

"Absolutely," he told her. "Whatever my baby wants, my baby gets."

Alexis was once again was surprised at his demeanor. "Okay, that works. There's a lot of stuff I'm going to have to go shopping for," she said, hinting that she needed money.

"Oh yeah, baby," he told her. "You know I gotta make sure you have everything you want and need for our getaway. How about we get together tomorrow night to hash out the details?" he asked her.

"Ok," she said. "I'll see you tomorrow night, baby."

"Cool," he responded. "Alright, baby, I got to go and try to finish some of these cases. But I'll call you tomorrow. I love you," he told her.

"I love you, too," Alexis responded.

The two hung up the phone and Alexis went to sleep dreaming of everything she was going to buy.

*

Alexis and Summer pulled up to Barber Park around 5 o'clock. Alexis had planned on getting to the park earlier than agreed so she could scope out the area just in case it was a set up. She made sure to carry her gun with her in case she had to use it. In the back of her mind, she was a little worried but, she didn't want Summer to know it. Parking her car, she and Summer started to check their surroundings.

"Damn, I didn't realize it was this many people here during the day like that," Summer said.

"Well, the busier that it is, the better," Alexis answered. "At least this way I know she won't try anything."

"That's true," Summer responded. "I still think you should have called that Detective, though," she told her.

"Damn, you sound worse than my daddy," Alexis joked with her friend.

"I wouldn't say all that," Summer said, laughing. "But seriously, though, how does this girl even know you?"

"Well, apparently she said she used to date him. And he threatened her," Alexis told her friend of what she knew.

"Um, okay. That doesn't make sense," Summer said. "If he dated her, then maybe he might be using her to get to you," Summer warned her.

"Well, shit, if he is, then both of them can get what they deserve. I'm not playing, Summer. I'm tired of running and I'm tired of fighting. He fucked my life up and he deserves the same treatment," Alexis said.

Summer, not wanting to argue with her friend, decided to change the subject. "Damn, I wonder where Tamika is. I called her mom before we late and she said she hadn't had a chance to go over there last night because she didn't get off work until late and she didn't want to wait to wake her up if she was asleep. I've tried to call her a couple of times and she didn't respond. You don't think anything happened to her, do you?" she asked.

"Nah. Maybe she's just got a lot to do right now. I don't even want to think about something like that," Alexis said.

"Well, she usually calls or texts. And you know she's the text queen. Shoot, you would think she would have at least done that by now. I'm going over to her house. I think we should do that when we leave here," Summer decided.

"Yea, that's not a bad idea. Especially if her mom is working crazy hours," Alexis agreed. "So hopefully this girl comes soon and then we can ride over there."

"Well, yea, we been here almost 20 minutes already," Summer remarked. "Do you want to just get out and walk around?" she asked her friend.

"Yeah," Alexis said. "That way we can spot her. She said that she would be on the benches by the playground."

The two girls got off the car and walked towards the playground area. Alexis made sure that she had her gun in her pocket. She really didn't like carrying it around, especially in large crowds, but given the situation, she deemed it necessary. The girls sat there and talked, passing time for 30 minutes. Close to 6 o'clock,

Alexis looked up to hear someone calling her name. She recognized the girl but she couldn't remember from where.

Summer sat quiet but her eyes locked on Ariane.

"Hey," Ariane said to Alexis.

"Hey," Alexis responded.

"I thought it was just going to be me and you?" Ariane asked, motioning toward Summer.

"Oh no, you not gonna have my girl here by herself," Summer responded.

"Chill out," Alexis told her angry friend. "So what's up? What you got to talk to me about?"

Ariane sat down on the bench and looked around. "I was dating Jayshawn right before he got locked up."

"Well, right before he got locked up, he was with that bitch Keisha," Alexis responded. "Wait a minute," Alexis said "Did you come over to the house while Keisha was there?"

Ariane was surprised that Alexis remembered that. "Yeah," she responded. "He had text me and told me that there was some girl there that wouldn't leave him alone," she responded. She couldn't let Alexis know that she was caught off guard so she had to play it cool. "He told me that he wasn't with her and that she was his baby mama."

"Well, I guess that part was true," Alexis said, listening to Ariane's version of the story.

"I just didn't know he was still sleeping with her. Trust me, had I known, I wouldn't have done half of everything I did for him," she told her. She really did regret some of the things that she'd done for Jayshawn's love so she wasn't lying to Alexis on that.

"So why should she believe anything that you have to say?" Summer asked her. "For all we know, you could be working with him to try to get her," she said.

"You have every right to not trust me," Ariane said. "But knowing what I know now, I want to do what's right. Knowing what you went through, justice needs to be served."

"And what do you get from this? Why are you so eager to help me all of a sudden?" Alexis asked.

Ariane worked up some tears and began her story. "When Jayshawn and I met, everything was cool. He was sweet, and I mean, I knew he had a record. I didn't have any reason not to believe him when he said that he just had a troubled past. His family seemed like they really didn't want him around." Much of what she was saying was in fact true, so it wasn't hard for her to be emotional. "Like I said, everything was fine until one day I was at his house and we got into an argument. The next thing I know, he hauled off and hit me. I didn't think he was capable of doing anything like that. He called me and apologized and said he had never hit a female before and that he was upset because his mother told him that she didn't want him around the house anymore. So I figured given the situation, that he was just upset. But then after that, he continuously abused me," she told Alexis.

Alexis suddenly remembered where she knew her from but she kept quiet, wondering if Ariane would mention that Alexis had witnessed her being beaten before.

"Well, anyway, everything was fine for a while until one day it just got too bad and the next thing you know, he hit me so hard I couldn't see out of my eye for a week. I felt so stupid because he would always call me and apologize and say that he didn't mean it. And I believed him. I listened to him so much that my own family called me names for messing with him," she whispered.

Tears begin to fall from Ariane's face as she thought about all of the times that Jayshawn abused her. Controlling her anger so as not to let Alexis see it, she continued. "I gave up everything. My entire family stopped communicating with me. Everybody said I was stupid. I even went to visit him in prison. I put money on his books, I did whatever he asked. I paid his lawyer. And the last time I went to see him, he used me. One of the guards in the prison used me for sex. It was his payment to turn the other way so that Jayshawn could escape."

Alexis' eyes grew larger at the news that she was hearing. "Wait a minute," she said. "Let me make sure I got this straight,"

Alexis said. "So you saw Jayshawn in prison and went to go visit him and he made you fuck somebody else so that he could escape?" she asked, just to make sure she'd heard correctly.

"Yeah," Ariane answered. She made sure to cover all our bases just in case Alexis or the police went back and saw the records from visitation. "He didn't have anybody and he was always writing me, telling me how much he loved me and how much he had changed since he'd been in prison. But I'm the fool that didn't know he was promising me to another man as payment for him getting out."

"This shit is fuckin crazy," Summer said.

"I know," Ariane told her. "I don't see how he could let somebody do that to me. I got raped in a damn storage closet; all for this nigga," she said. "Now I'm getting anonymous phone calls from him saying that if I go to the police, he's going to kill me. It's like he's lost his mind. I'm scared and I don't know what else to do," she said.

"Okay, so I still don't understand why you're calling me. I mean, aside from warning me that he's coming or rather that he's here, what do you need me for? What do you want with me?" Alexis asked.

"My brother called me and told me that Jayshawn showed up to his house. He's been hanging out there for the last couple of months. I can't let anything happen to my brother," Ariane explained.

"Then why the hell haven't you called the cops?" Alexis asked.

"You don't know Jayshawn. If I call the cops, he'll kill him. My brother is all I have left," Ariane explain to her.

"I get all of it, but I'm still trying to understand why you're telling me all of this," Alexis said.

"Because I think he killed your boyfriend."

Summer looked up at Alexis. "How do you know that for sure?" Summer asked.

"I don't know for sure," Ariane said. "But I remember him saying something about him when he was in there," she explained.

"Okay, so what do you want?" Alexis asked. "I mean, what he did to you was messed up, but what he did to me almost killed me. He's psycho. And if he never breathes another day on this earth, I will be more than happy," she said.

"And that's why I contacted you," Ariane told her. "I can easily call the cops. But he could hurt my family. I want to put him away. Permanently," she said suggestively.

Summer looked at her as if she had lost her mind. "I know you're not asking my best friend to do what I think you're asking her to do," she said. "You gotta be out your fuckin' mind. Alexis, I really hope you're not stupid enough to listen to this dumb bitch," she fussed.

Ariane was trying to keep her composure but this girl was starting to get on her nerves. She wanted to choke her out right there but she had to continue to play the part and remember the overall goal was to make Jayshawn suffer. "Look," Ariane said. "I'm not asking you to do anything you don't want to do. But I know I'm not the only one that he's hurt. It's up to you what you do with it," she told her.

Alexis looked at her friend Summer.

"Are you sure that you really want to do this?" Summer asked her.

Alexis thought about it. "I remember you," she told Ariane. "I remember that you came over one day when I was outside and Jayshawn snatched you up. I didn't know that he was beating you," she said quietly.

Summer grew quiet and looked on. Ariane was once again surprised that Alexis remembered her. Not wanting to blow her cover, she pretended to be sad. "Yeah, I remember that day," Ariane said.

"I'm sorry you had to go through that," Alexis told her. She thought about everything that had happened to her two years ago and the fear that she had been living with. She remembered seeing the fear on Ariane's face that day. "Give me his address," Alexis told her.

"Are you sure?" Ariane asked, faking concern.

Alexis looked at her with a serious expression. "Give me his address."

*

Alexis and Summer pulled up to Tamika's apartment complex. The two had hardly spoken since they left the park. Alexis' mind was racing with thoughts about everything that Ariane told her. Summer didn't trust Ariane and wanted to confront her but because Alexis seemed interested in what she had to say, she sided with her friend and kept quiet. She made a mental note to get the info on the girl later. But for the time being, they were concerned about their friend.

"I hope I still have my spare key," Summer said. Tamika had given her to spare key to her apartment when she first moved in. Summer looked around in her purse to find it. She pulled out several keys that were not on a key ring. "I know one of these has got to be it," she said.

The girls got out the car and walked up the two flights of steps to their friend's apartment. Summer started trying the keys to unlock the door while Alexis look around the building. She heard someone open her door and looked over to see an elderly white lady looking at them.

"Are y'all looking for the nice young lady that lives there?" she heard the lady ask.

"Yes ma'am," Alexis told her. "She's a friend of ours. Have you seen her?"

"I haven't. She usually comes over and walks my dog for me. I saw a guy leaving there a few days ago. He looked like he was in a hurry," she informed her.

Alexis looked at Summer with a look of panic on her face. "Summer, hurry up. You gotta open the door."

"Is everything okay?" the elderly lady asked.

"I hope so." Alexis said under her breath. "Thank you, ma'am," she told the lady.

Summer finally got the right key to unlock the door. Alexis pulled her gun out of her purse just in case. Summer opened the door and the two walked into the apartment.

"Mika?" Summer called out. They didn't see anything in the hallway. Sandra walked into the kitchen area while Alexis walked towards the living room.

"Oh my God!" Summer heard Alexis cry out. "Oh my God. Tamika, no! Call 911!"

Summer ran towards Alexis' voice and saw the horror her friend saw; their friend was lying dead on the couch.

*

Alexis sat on the curb outside of her friend's apartment complex. The last 20 minutes kept playing through her mind. All she could see was Tamika's body slumped over on the couch and lifeless. Alexis was horrified. She remembered Summer calling the cops and all she could do was break down and cry. The police were taking statements but Alexis had hardly said two words. Summer was telling the officers everything that she remembered since they got there.

Detective Williams walked toward Alexis. "Ms. Thomas," he said. "I hate that yet again you are having to deal with another loss. From what your friend was telling me, you three were really close?" he asked her.

Alexis heard him talking but she just couldn't respond. Detective William saw the shock that Alexis was in and sat down next to her on the curb. "I know there are no words that I can say that will bring your friend back. I know you all were very close and I know it's repetitive for me to say that I hate that you have to keep going through these things. But rest assured, Ms. Thomas; we will get him. Your friend told us about the neighbor that saw Mr. Cheston leaving the apartment," he told her. "We have an APB out on him now in the surrounding area."

Alexis lifted her head to look at Detective Williams and her body slumped over. She broke down crying. "I can't take this," she wept. "I can't take it anymore. Why is all of this happening to me? Why can't he just leave me alone? He killed his own sister. He killed my friend! Why?! It's not fair! And now she's gone. I should've forgiven her a long time ago. I was just being stubborn. I'm so sorry, Tamika," she cried. "I'm so sorry." Alexis cried harder and harder.

Summer seeing her friend upset came over and sat down. "It's okay," she told her. "It's okay, Lexis. She knows that you're sorry. She forgave you a long time ago. The one thing about you two that you had in common is that both of you were stubborn. But trust me, she knew that you were sorry. It's going to be ok."

It was at that moment that Alexis saw Tamika's mother pull up. Detective Williams had contacted her to let her know that someone had found her daughter's body and needed her to come immediately. She got out of her car and ran over towards Alexis and Summer. When she saw the tears on their faces she knew her baby was gone.

Summer ran over to her mom. "I'm so sorry," she told her. She grabbed her and hugged her tight as Tamika's mother wailed in the middle of the parking lot. Rage took over Alexis. She looked at the detective who was now writing in his notepad.

"He can't get away with this," she whispered.

"I'm sorry, what was that?" he asked her.

"He can't get away with this," she said louder. "He is taking everything from me. He's taking my life, my friends, and my boyfriend. He can't get away with this."

Detective walked her over to a secluded area to keep her from drawing attention to her. "You've got to try to calm down, Ms. Thomas. As I said before, we have an APB out in the area," he said.

It was then that Alexis remembered Ariane gave her the address to her brother's apartment. "I know where he is," she told the detective.

Confuse the detective looked around. "What do you mean?"

"I know where he is," she said again. "Earlier today, I met with his ex-girlfriend. She had come over one day when I lived in the complex where he lived. She told me that he's hiding out at her brother's apartment. I have the address," Alexis said, pulling the piece of paper from her pocket and handing it to him.

He looked at the address and saw that it was less than 5 minutes from their location. Detective Williams pulled out his cell phone and hit a speed dial button and made a call. "This is Williams," he said. "I need all available units to 415 Marshall Street. I repeat, I need all available units to 415 Marshall Street. Be advised that the suspect is armed and dangerous," he informed dispatch before hanging up. "Ms. Thomas, I need you to tell me everything you know about this young lady," he said.

Alexis filled him in on everything that Ariane had told her when they met. She told the detective about Ariane dating Jayshawn around the time that she was kidnapped and how he was beating her. She told him of how Jayshawn had used Ariane as a pawn to escape from prison and the correctional officer that turned the other way so that he could get away. She filled him in on all of the details about Ariane believing that he killed Collin and how he'd threatened her family. When she was done telling him everything, Detective Williams was very much surprised.

"Ms. Thomas, thank you. What I need you to do is get somewhere safe for the time being and wait for my call. Can you do that?" he asked her.

"Yes," she said.

"Good. Go," he said. "Go now."

Alexis went to Summer and the two got in the car quickly and headed to the Four Seasons Hotel where Alexis and Malik usually met. She called the Malik's phone to cancel their plans for the evening.

*

CHAPTER TEN

Detective Williams was staged a block away from 415 Marshall Street where Jayshawn was located. He and other officers were waiting for his captain's instructions. Careful not to tip Jayshawn off, the detective had several undercover cars posted close to the area. His captain gave his instructions over the radio to move in, but cautiously. Detective Williams gave the green light and they begin to move in.

Guns drawn, several officers and SWAT team members ran to the apartment complex that Jayshawn was known to be in. Detective Williams posted the officers to every area of the building to prevent him from escaping. He gave the nod for one of the SWAT members to knock on the door.

Boom! Boom! Boom!

"Jayshawn Cheston, this is Greensboro police. We know you're in there. Open up!" Defective Williams yelled. He heard a loud thud and new Jayshawn was on the move to run. Stepping back, the SWAT member used his battering ram to bust down the door.

Several agents bombarded the apartment.

Bang! Bang! Bang! Bang!

Shots were fired from the apartment and a few offices retreated. Detective Williams watched one officer fall. SWAT ran in and chased after Jayshawn after the firing stopped. Catching him running out the corner of his eye, the detective aimed.

"Freeze!" he yelled. Jayshawn fired another shot and hid behind the bedroom door. Detective Williams took cover behind the pillar in the living room. "Come on, Jayshawn! Just give up. Don't let it end this way. You're clearly out-numbered in this situation," he said.

"Fuck you!" he heard from the room. "I'm not going back."

Another officer closed in on the room as the detective tried to talk him down. "You gotta go back. You ain't going alone, don't worry. We already got the officer that you worked with and are charging him with rape," he lied.

They had not actually charged Officer Ricks yet, and wouldn't until they had Jayshawn in custody. They couldn't charge him with rape, but they could charge him with aiding an inmate's escape.

"What the fuck are you talkin about, nigga?" Jayshawn asked.

"Your girlfriend told us everything. She told me how you used her to get free. We know about Rick's sleeping with her in exchange for payment for you getting out," the detective yelled.

"Man, that's bullshit!" Jayshawn said. "I told you, I'm NOT going back."

"Come on, man, and make this easy. We can do this all day."

Detective Williams was stalling, giving the officer time to throw the tear gas that was in his hand. The room filled with the gas, giving the detective the advantage he needed. He rushed in, punching Jayshawn and knocking the gun out of his hand. He slapped on the handcuffs and yanked him out of the room.

"I told you that you were outnumbered, stupid muthafucka," he said. "Time to take you back." Jayshawn struggled to get out of the detective's grip, but was no match. "Jayshawn Cheston, you are under arrest for the escape from Hoke County facility, for conspiracy to solicit prostitution, and for the murders of Collin Strong, Jr., and Tamika Blackwell. You have the right to remain silent. Anything you say can and will be used against you in a court of law. You have the right to an attorney. If you cannot afford an attorney, one will be provided for you. Do you understand the rights I have just read to you?"

Jayshawn said nothing as the detective walked him to the car. All he could think was who the fuck set him up. He remembered the detective saying that Ricks had been charged with raping his girlfriend. *This bitch set me up!* he thought to himself. *So these muthafuckas want to play me?* he thought. He just knew that Ariane and Ricks had set him up to get caught. He had thoughts of the phrase of a woman scorned and became furious. *She fuckin' another nigga but crying to me about how she lost the baby that probably wasn't even mine. They probably been fuckin behind my back the whole time.* Somehow, someway, he was going to get both of them back.

Detective Williams threw Jayshawn into the back of the squad car. "Watch your head," he said, banging it against the car door on purpose before closing the car door. Detective Williams pulled out his cell phone and made a phone call. "Ms. Thomas. This is Detective Williams. We got him," he said.

What no one saw was Ariane sitting down the street in her car watching the entire scene, smiling.

*

"Oh my God, thank you!" Alexis said with tears in her eyes. She hung up her cell phone. "They got him!" she told her friend Summer. She and Summer were staying in a room at the Four Seasons awaiting Detective Williams' call.

"They picked him up from exactly where Ariane said he would be, at her brother's apartment," she said.

"So… it's over?" Summer asked her.

"Yeah," Alexis sighed, relieved. "It's over."

The two hugged each other tight thinking about their lost friend. "Tamika and Collin will get justice," Alexis said. "I guess Ariane was on our side."

"Yeah," Summer said. "I guess."

Alexis picked up her phone so that she could call her father. When he didn't answer, she left him a voicemail. "Hey, Dad, it's me," she said. "I'm just letting you know that I received a phone call from Detective Williams. It's over. They have him in custody. I just wanted to call you and tell you the good news. Give me a call when you get the message. I love you."

She threw her phone inside her purse. "Wow. It's almost unreal. This shit is finally over."

"Hell yeah," her friend agreed. "I'm glad you're okay. I couldn't have imagined losing both my best friends, man," she said.

"I know. I hate that Tamika is gone," Alexis told her solemnly. "But after the last few months, I've definitely learned that I can't hold grudges anymore. I think I got something I need to do," Alexis said. She pulled her cell phone back out her bag and called her therapist's office. "Yes, this is Alexis Thomas," she said. "I need to see if Dr. Rhimes can see me today."

The receptionist put her on hold and came back a few minutes later. "Yes ma'am. We do have an opening today. If you can make it here, he has availability within an hour."

"That's fine. I'll see you guys then," Alexis said. She hung up her phone and got her purse and keys. "I'm going to go to my therapist's office," Alexis told Summer. "I'll hit you up in a few. Thank you so much for everything that you've done for me these last few weeks. I know you didn't have to and I know you've dealt with my being stubborn, but I really appreciate it."

"Girl, bye. That's what I'm here for. We're sisters. Go handle your business. I'm about to go home and relax. This has been a crazy day. I just wanna sleep for a while. So go handle your business and I'll holler at you in a few." Summer gathered her things and walked out the door.

Alexis sat down on the edge of the bed and thought about everything that had happened within the last few days. She thought about Collin and about losing her best friend. It hurt her more than she knew. Feeling the tears sting her eyes, she let them fall. She cried for her friend and for her ex-boyfriend, knowing that he would never be able to fulfill his dreams. She decided that it was time for her to turn over a new leaf. Feeling as if God gave her a second chance, she let go of all the pain and anger that she had been holding it.

"Thank you, God," she said out loud. "Thank you for opening my eyes and for saving me," she said. She wiped her tears and grabbed her phone once again. She called Malik but he didn't answer. She realized it was midafternoon and figured he was either in court or busy at the firm. When she got his voicemail, she decided that was the best way to tell him goodbye.

"Hey, Malik, it's Alexis. I know this is sudden and probably something you weren't expecting, but I had to let you know that I can't see you anymore. Although I had lot of fun with you, and although I care about you, I can't lie to you and say that I love you. I'm sorry if I'm springing this on you, but I really need to focus on me. There's a lot of things that I didn't tell you, and a lot of things that I'm scared to tell you for fear of judgement. So please forgive me for ending it this way, but I have to say goodbye," she said.

She hung up her phone and walked out the door. No sooner had she opened the door than she staggered from someone hitting her in her face. She looked up to see a woman punching her repeatedly. Caught off guard, Alexis fell to the ground.

"You home wrecking bitch!" she heard the woman yelling. "You didn't think I would find you? You nasty hoe! I had you muthafuckas followed! Stay the fuck away from my husband!" the lady screamed. "You fucked up my life!" The woman continuously attacked her, throwing heavy blows. Alexis lay on the ground trying to fight back.

The woman stood over her, hair disheveled. She looked down at Alexis and told her, "If I catch you near my husband again, I will kill you. And that's a promise." She kicked Alexis in the head as hard as possible. Alexis looked at her running down the hall before she lost consciousness.

When Alexis came to, she was in the hospital. She opened her eyes to see Summer across the room. "What happened?" she whispered to her friend. Summer turned around quickly to see Alexis awake.

"Girl, you just attract trouble like a magnet," Summer fussed at her. "That nigga's wife that you've been fuckin with came over to the hotel room. They caught it all on security cameras. They found her not too far from the hotel and arrested her. I told you about fuckin with married men," she said.

"Summer, don't start. I'm tired and my head is killing me," she told her friend, trying to clear her throat.

"Lex, I wouldn't have to start if you wouldn't keep making such stupid decisions," she told her. "This man's wife came after you. You gotta realize you messing with somebody family. Hell, he's old enough to be your daddy."

"I know that," Alexis spat. "That's why I broke it off with him today."

"You broke it off with him, and yet his wife came after you anyway?" Summer asked her sarcastically.

"Yes. Right before I left the hotel room, I called him and left him a voicemail letting him know I couldn't see him anymore. The fact that she came to the hotel room was purely coincidental. She said she had us followed so I'm guessing she knew beforehand," Alexis explained.

"Uh huh, if you say so. I'm going down the hall to get the nurse to let her know that you're awake." Summer left the room and Alexis closed her eyes. She opened her eyes when she heard the door creaking.

Malik entered the room looking miserable. "Hey, princess," he said. Looking at her and seeing the pain that she was in, he grimaced. "I am so sorry," he said to her. "I didn't know that my wife even knew what you looked like," he pleaded. "Security got her on camera and they said that they arrested her. Apparently, she had a private investigator following us to the hotel. I'm so sorry, princess. I hope you can forgive me. I told her I didn't want anything else to do with her. I love you."

At that moment, Summer entered the room with the nurse. "Oh hell no!" She said. "You got to go. Can y'all get security please?" she asked.

The nurse, looking confused, asked should she really get security.

"Yes," Summer said.

"No," Alexis said. "It's not necessary. Can you just give us a minute, please?" she asked.

Summer looked at her. "And you wonder why this kind of shit keeps happening," she said.

"Summer, just get the hell out!" she said. "I'm trying to handle this my way. You yelling and cussing is not helping the situation. Just go," she said.

"Okay. I'll be right outside," Summer, replied throwing up her hands in a fake surrender. "By the way, your dad called and said that he's flying in and should be here tonight."

Hearing that her father was coming into town early only made Alexis' stomach hurt. "Great," she said. "Now I gotta hear this from him, too," Summer and the nurse exited the room, leaving Malik and Alexis alone.

"Princess, what can I do to make this better?" he asked her.

"You can leave me alone," Alexis said quietly.

"What?" He asked.

"I take it you didn't get my voicemail. Look, Malik, I know I told you that I loved you the other day, but I don't," she said. "I would be lying to you if I said that I cared for you to that extreme. I'm sorry. I didn't mean to string you along but I've gotta think about me from now on. I'm about to graduate. And with everything going on here, I need to leave. I need to start over fresh. And you have a family," she said.

"You have a wife that clearly loves you because if she didn't, she wouldn't have come after me today. The fact that I got attacked lets me know I can't be with you. We'll never be able to be together because I will always be looking over my shoulder to see if your wife is coming after me. Do you know she threatened to kill me if I saw you again?" she asked. "The mere fact that you're here in this room now is putting you at risk. I can't do it. I'm sorry. We could never be together because there would be too many people against our relationship. I don't want to be with someone that I have to hide in corners with," she said.

"But I don't want to hide you," he said. "I don't care about her anymore, princess. I care about you. You don't love me right now? Okay, that's fine. But get to know me. Be with me. I know you'll love me just as much as I love you," he said.

Alexis was starting to get annoyed but remained calm. "I can't. My plans were to leave Greensboro after I graduated. If I stay, I would be staying strictly for you and I know I wouldn't be happy. I'm going to grad school in Atlanta."

"Ok," he said. "I have a house in Atlanta. It's not like I can't come there." He was bargaining with her.

"So you don't see the problem with you being willing to jump up and run to Atlanta whenever I ask?" she said. "I don't want someone like that will be that way. As much fun as we had, I want someone that doesn't have to sacrifice everything for me and vice versa. Just please try to understand. I'm sorry, but I can't be with you," she said.

Malik looked at her defeated. "So is this how you really want to end it?" he asked.

"It's the only way," she said. "When I get out of here, I'll send you the gifts back that you gave me," she said so he would know she was clear about ending it.

Malik looked at her and shook his head. "No need to do that. I bought those for you because I wanted you to have them. Giving them back would only be a reminder of what I couldn't have. Take care, princess." He kissed her forehead and left the room.

Summer came in quiet. "You okay?" she asked.

"Yeah, I'm fine. I just told him I couldn't deal with him anymore. I can't risk my health or safety because I tore apart his family," she said.

"Well at least you recognize that," she sympathized. "Now, I need you to hurry up and get better so that we can get ready to walk across that stage, bitch!" she said, laughing.

Alexis chuckled. "Don't make me laugh; it hurts," she said.

"I know, my bad," Summer apologized. "Your dad's flight should be here in about an hour so, I'm going to go ahead and go pick him up from the airport. I'll be back shortly," she told her.

"Hey, do me a favor?" Alexis asked.

"Yeah, sure; wassup?" her friend asked.

"Look in my purse. There should be a notebook and a pen. Can you hand it to me?"

Summer looked into the purse, pulling out the items Alexis needed and handed them to her. "There you go. You want me to pull the tray over so that you can write?" she asked.

"Yeah, thanks," Alexis said.

"No problem, girl. I'll be back in a few." Summer left and Alexis began writing in her notebook.

Dear Dr. Rhimes,

Unfortunately I could not make it today for our last session. But I want to thank you for all of the help that you have given me. These last few weeks have been nothing short of crazy. But I'm learning to let go of the anger and to live for me. I did a LOT of things in my past and present that I regret, but knowing that I am about to graduate and start a new life in Atlanta makes things so much better. I have excelled in so many areas that I never thought possible and I have you to thank for that. Look at me. I am about to be a college graduate, with a degree in criminal justice, of all things. I'm a proud member of Delta, and I will be starting grad school at Clark Atlanta University in the fall. I'd never seen myself living the life that I am living currently. But I now know that I can't take it for granted, and that I must live each day to the fullest. I failed to tell you that Jayshawn escaped from prison because I didn't want to give him any power in our sessions, but he has since been caught and he is being charged with the murder of Collin and my best friend Tamika. I know I am growing as a person because I dealt with all of that on my own. I hate that they died because of his hatred for me, but I know that justice will prevail. I wanted to take the time out to thank you. You've helped me in so many ways that you don't even understand. I hope that one day I may be able to help people as much as you have helped me.

Sincerely,

Alexis.

*

Alexis stood in line at the Coliseum awaiting the President to call her name for graduation. She looked over to see her best friend standing two spots in front of her. Almost instantly, Summer looked back and smiled at her friend. Motioning the thumbs up, she began smiling, too.

"Graduation, bitch," Summer mouthed. Her name was called and Summer walked across the stage cheering loudly as Alexis cheered loudly from the steps. Summer accepted her degree and proceeded to walk across the stage.

"Alexis Thomas," she heard the president call.

Alexis climbed the stairs and walked across the stage while her family and friends stood in the audience cheering her on. Her father had a bullhorn he honked that resonated through the room. An entire section of her sorority sisters stood, making the call, and she threw her sign in the air. Alexis was on cloud nine. Beaming from ear to ear, she jumped off the stage and embraced her best friend in a hug.

The two held their degrees in the air. "This is for Collin and Tamika," Alexis said.

"For Collin and Tamika," Summer agreed. They walk towards their seats, sitting down and waiting for the remainder of the graduation ceremony to be completed. Alexis sat, barely able to pay attention to the commencement speech because she was so excited. She felt her phone vibrate. She had snuck her phone into the Coliseum in her bra.

The school administration told everyone that they weren't allowed to bring their cell phones on the Coliseum floor, however just as every other graduating class had done, almost all of the students had snuck their cell phones in some kind of way. She pulled her phone out to see she had two text messages; one from Henderson and the other from Detective Williams. She opened the message from Henderson first.

Henderson: Congratulations on graduating, big head. Look up and to your right 6th row.

Alexis grinned, looking up to see Henderson sitting and looking at her. It really touched her that he came to support her.

Alexis: Wow. I can't believe ur here. Let me find out u tryna get back with me.

Henderson: Lol. Pay attention, big head.

Alexis smiled at Henderson and blew him a kiss. She opened the message from the detective.

Det.Williams: Good afternoon, Alexis. Just wanted to let you know that Jayshawn's court hearing is scheduled for Tuesday at 9am. They're asking you to be present for testimony regarding his charges.

"What's the matter?" Summer whispered leaning forward.

Alexis leaned forward so her friend could hear her. "Nothing. The detective texted me with the court date."

"Oh, ok. You need me to go with you?" she asked.

"No, I'll be fine. Besides, dad will be here. I told him about everything and that there was a possibility that I would have to go to court, so he's prepared to say a few extra days. Plus, we have to pack up the rest of my apartment and fly out to Atlanta to go apartment shopping," she told her friend.

"Cool," Summer answered

"Oh guess who's here. Henderson," Alexis said with a smile.

Summer gave her an eye roll. "I guess he's better than Malik," she said.

"Whatever," she hissed.

It was time for all of the students to rise. "I present to you, the graduating class of 2005," the president stated. The students began cheering along with their family and friends, tossing their hats in the air.

"We did it, bitch!" Alexis said

"Yes, we did." The two hugged and went to join their parents.

New life here I come, Alexis said to herself. She and Summer began walking to the future.

*

Ariane walked into the Guilford County Courthouse for Jayshawn's trial. She had spoken with the attorney who told her they may need her to testify. She walked into the courtroom to see the judge was dismissing another case and another case was being called. She looked over to see Alexis, Summer, Henderson and an older gentleman awaiting on the bench across from the one she sat in. The courtroom doors open and Jayshawn entered in cuffs. Ariane smirked, thinking about the torture that she'd endured and the years of torture he was about to endure in prison. She had contacted a cousin of hers that knew people that could make his life miserable.

"Now seeing case number 69375," the bailiff called. "The state of North Carolina versus Jayshawn Cheston."

The courtroom doors opened and in walked three well-dressed black men. Alexis and Summer both turned to see who'd entered the room and Alexis looked struck. Frowning, Alexis quickly turned back around. *What was that about?* Ariane asked herself. Before she could give it a second thought, the judge banged his gavel.

"Court is now in session. Counselors, I am understanding the defendant is an escapee from Hoke County Correctional Facility and during his time out, has murdered two promising students, one of whom was his relative, Collin Strong Jr. and Tamika Blackwell. Is the complete representation here today?" he asked.

"Yes, Your Honor. Luther Franklin representing Tamika Blackwell."

Alexis saw Malik stand.

"Malik Davis, representing the defendant, Jayshawn Cheston."

Alexis felt her chest tightening. "This can't be happening," she whispered. Henderson and her father looked at her, confused.

"Alexis, you have to say something," Summer whispered loudly.

Palms sweating, Alexis stood slowly. "Excuse me Your Honor," she said. "This case can't proceed."

"State your name," the judge instructed her.

"Alexis Thomas, Your Honor. I'm sorry for interrupting, but the case is compromised."

The judge looked at her over his glasses. "Yes, I see you are one of the witnesses testifying against the defendant today and were one of his victims. You say that that the case has been compromised. Now how is that?"

Alexis looked back at her father and Henderson looking at her, wondering what was going on.

"Young lady, I'm waiting," the judge said.

Malik's eyes widened when she spoke.

"I know the defense attorney...intimately," she answered in barely a whisper, feeling eyes on her.

The door burst open and a woman ran in screaming. "You muthafucka!" she yelled, raising a gun and opening fire.

Alexis fell to the ground and heard a man yelling.

"Someone call 911!"

To be continued…

Text ROYALTY to 42828 to get a notification for when PART THREE is available!

THANK YOU

I can't believe that I am at this point in my life where I am releasing my third book. Thank you so much for all that have supported me in my dream. I started doing this as a hobby, but to know that you all love these stories means so much. I am blessed to be with such a wonderful company. Royalty Publishing House ROCKS!!!

Of course, I have to thank my Heavenly Father. I know many don't understand thanking God for being able to write urban erotica, but it is a gift that He has given me that I am so grateful for to tell MY STORY.

My husband Michael, thank you for supporting my dream. You pushed me to tell my story despite everyone else's opinions. I love you so much and admire you for the man that you are, my Honey Bunches of Oats.

My children, I thank God for you each day and I know you all are too small to understand, but you motivate mommy on a daily. I love you and do this for you.

My parents, I know you're not big on these types of books but I know that you are big on supporting me, and I thank you for that. Words can't express how much I love you all.

To my sorority sisters of Zeta Phi Beta Sorority, Incorporated, don't be mad I made her a Delta in the book. Lol. But seriously, I could not have a better group of sisters. Shout out to Spr. 2005 DECks of ChaoZ.

My Sweetheart Sisters, Gabbie, Pokey, Peanut, Toya, Terrika, Chae, and especially my HAM, I love y'all so much. Ham, I hope you are happy with this story. Lol. No worries, part 3 will be out soon so don't beat me.

For all my friends, my bestie Jessie, my ls Dawn, my Hags Steve and Keisha (no relation to the one in the book) love my boos. My sis JaNell and brother Doug, love y'all.

My sisters and brothers, Lloyd, Kiaren, Kimani, and Kise, love y'all NO MATTER WHAT. My big sis Brandi, you are such an inspiration and a FIGHTER and I love you.

My FFCS Fam, thank you so much for all your support, and in letting me sell my books and always promoting. Special shout out to B Daht (who gave me my name!), Coe, Chuck, love y'all man.

Most importantly, to my fans, thank you, Thank You, THANK YOU for all your support. Y'all are the reason I do this!

Stay tuned for more. Peace and love y'all! *Confessions of a Dope Boy 2* coming soon!

First Lady K's Contact Info

https://www.facebook.com/authorfirstladyk

Twitter: @author1stladyk

Instagram: @authorfirstladyk

Email: authorfirstladyk@yahoo.com

Website: www.authorfirstladyk.com

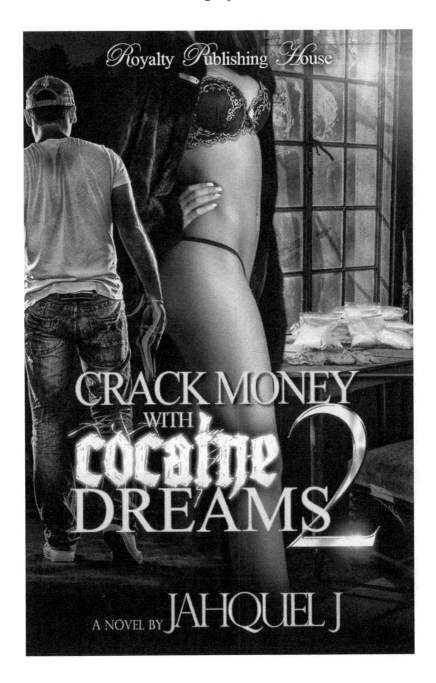

Coming April 10th!

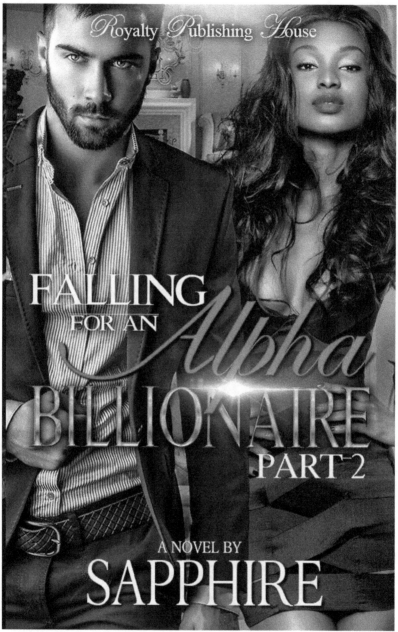

Coming soon!

First Lady K

Coming Soon!

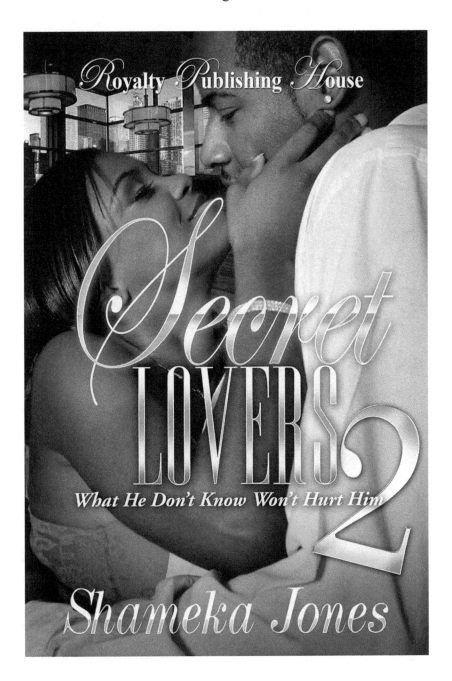

Royalty Publishing House

Secret
LOVERS 2
What He Don't Know Won't Hurt Him

Shameka Jones

It Ain't Trickin' If You Got It 2

Coming SOON! A ROYALTY series! Make sure to keep your eyes
open for this EPIC series!

A NOVEL BY
JAHQUEL J. & QUIANA NICOLE

Coming SOON! A ROYALTY series! Make sure to keep your eyes open for this EPIC series!

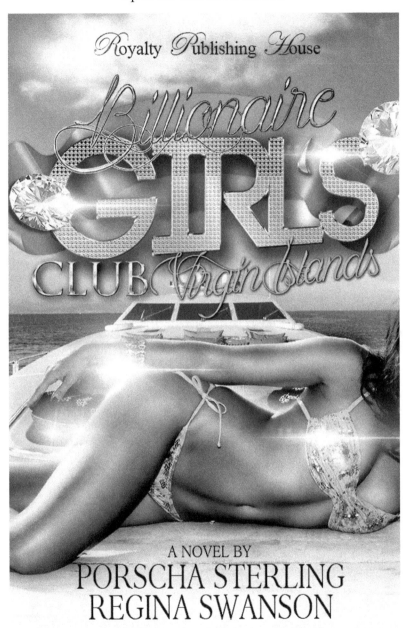

Coming SOON! A ROYALTY series! Make sure to keep your eyes open for this EPIC series!

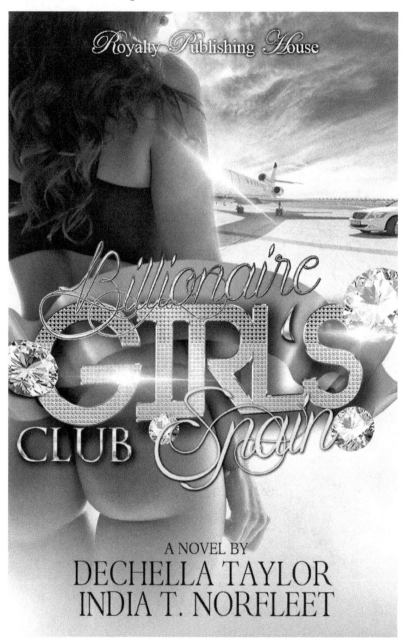

Text ROYALTY to 42828 to join our mailing list!

ROYALTY is looking for aspiring authors in the areas of Urban Fiction, Urban Romance & Interracial Romance. If you are looking for an independent publishing company, submit the first 3 – 4 chapters of your completed manuscript to submissions@royaltypublishinghouse.com.

CPSIA information can be obtained
at www.ICGtesting.com
Printed in the USA
LVHW031828220120
644443LV00013B/804